Understand Me, Sugar

Stories by Jane V. Blunschi

~ The Cypress & Pine Fiction Series ~

UNDERSTAND ME, SUGAR
Jane V. Blunschi

All Stories © Jane V. Blunschi
© 2017 Yellow Flag Press

Cover Art: "St. Roch Chapel Cures"
© 2009 by Michael Brownlee

Author Photo Credit: Steph Shinabery

Layout and Design by W. Scott Thomason
Cover Design by J. Bruce Fuller

First Edition
February 2017

ISBN 978-1-365-64068-1

Yellow Flag Press
2275 S. Bascom Ave. #702
Campbell, CA 95008

www.yellowflagpress.com

YFP-138

Praise for *Understand Me, Sugar*

Funny and tragic and leavened by faith, *Understand Me, Sugar* wages for hope. Blunschi has crafted a rich cast of characters who bide and break in the name of transformation, "grazing the dark interior" to expose (if not detangle) the messy threads of desire and suffering. You will want to experience this well-written collection of stories more than once, to return and linger with its difficult questions about self-discovery and the things that prevent us from feeling connected across the joys and disasters of living.

—Geffrey Davis, author of *Revising the Storm*

Understand Me, Sugar invites the reader to follow some very appealing characters over some very dubious moral terrain. We might be appalled by their choices, even more by how we identify with them, and still further by how they make us laugh. If these stories weren't so intelligent, they would be guilty pleasures.

—Padma Viswanathan, author of *The Ever After of Ashwin Rao* and *The Toss of a Lemon*

Jane Blunschi doesn't flinch in her storytelling, and the result is a collection of searingly honest tales that lay bare a full-throated humanity. Her characters, whether they're trying to find a sperm donor or talk to their newly found biological mother or just get drunk, are smart, funny, and gut-wrenchingly familiar. As Blunschi's voice slips under the skin of these people, and flows in their bloodstreams, the reader can't help but think, *this could be me.*

—Lucy Jane Bledsoe, author of *A Thin Bright Line* and *The Big Bang Symphony*

Jane Blunschi is one of the sassiest writers I know. She goes deep, she goes dark, she goes wicked, sly, cut-your-eyes-sideways funny. With wit and insight, Blunschi evokes contemporary women, their lives, relationships, and concerns, with as keen an edge as any writer working today. *Understand Me, Sugar* is a pure, unadulterated delight.

—Rilla Askew, author of *Kind of Kin*

Contents

Understand Me, Sugar

This collection is dedicated to my mother, who is praying for me.

The Goods

I met Amy last year at a Christmas party for the alumni of the sorority my girlfriend Kim belonged to in college. Not the whole sorority, just the sisters in her year who turned out to be gay. The ones who headed up the chapter's touch football games for charity and managed to make it through undergrad without engagement rings or pregnancy scares. Five or six women, plus a rotating cast of significant others, met up once a year at an Italian restaurant for drinks and fried appetizers and conversation. Amy was there with her partner that night, a reserved, soft-butch corporate attorney named Sally. Kim introduced us and then she and Sally talked about mutual funds while Amy showed me a bunch of pictures of their twin daughters on her phone. These twins were the reason they hadn't been to the party in six years. "We've been on lockdown since the day they were born," Amy said. Kim and I had just started talking about getting pregnant, and I told Amy how nervous I was. "I have no idea what I'm doing." I said. "I'm kind of afraid."

"I get it." Amy said. "Sally and I had to work so hard for this. We were willing to do anything. Except adoption. There was no way I was doing that."

"No?"

"No way. I wanted my own child." That last remark gave me pause, but I was full of booze and fried artichokes, so I decided to ignore it. At the end of the night we all agreed that we should get together for a double date sometime and not let another year go by before we saw each other again.

Amy was at the party again this year, and she was different. She looked thinner, and snug designer jeans and cowboy boots replaced the boring navy pantsuit she had worn the night we met. We hadn't had that double date after all, and when I asked about Sally, she rolled her eyes. "That's over. We split up six months ago." She asked Kim and I if we had any single friends and then she asked if we were still thinking about having a baby. "Oh, yes," I said. "We never got together to talk about that. I meant to call you."

She made a horrified face at Kim and I. "You haven't *started?* You need to get this show on the road, honey."

"I know," I said. "I know. The women in my family are good at having babies, though. When I turned sixteen my mother told me not to stand too close to a man unless I was ready to change my name to 'Mommy.'" Kim and I laughed, but Amy's expression had gone from horrified to grave.

"It took us five solid years. Sally did six rounds of IVF and it was too much." She air quoted the "too much" in a bitchy way that made me think her relationship with Sally hadn't ended very nicely. "And then I tried and we got pregnant right away, which she never got over. It was worth it, though. It was all worth it for my little baby angels." Amy said that we should come over sometime, "So that we can really sit down and talk. I'll tell you everything you need to know." Amy said she needed to leave the party soon so that she could go over to Sally's and open the door on the Advent calendar with the twins before they went to sleep.

"So you and Sally are sharing custody?" Kim asked.

"Yeah, they're with her tonight. It's rough. We pretty much hate each other's guts right now. Sally and I, that is."

"I knew what you meant," I said.

I made Kim call Amy the next week to set up a time for us to drop by and visit. The idea of talking to Amy about where she got the other half of her kids' DNA made me nervous, but Kim reassured me. "It's fine, she *wants* to help, and she'll probably do most of the talking. After a glass or two of wine she's like a conversation freight train."

"Honestly, I think she's awful," I said. "Please don't set her up with any of our friends."

Standing at Amy's front door the next afternoon, I squeezed Kim's hand before she had a chance to knock. "In and out, okay? Tell her we have dinner reservations." We did not have dinner reservations.

"I got it, Carrie. Relax."

8

"I'm just uncomfortable, alright? "

"Smile, honey. She's helping us out."

Amy's twin daughters answered the door, and hand to God, curtsied and said "good afternoon" in adorable soprano harmony before showing us to the living room. They called us Miss Carrie and Miss Kim and brought us each a glass of water with lemon slices and said "yes, ma'am" and disappeared when Amy told them to go to their rooms and straighten up the toy box so that we could sit and talk.

"You really lucked out," I said. "Jane and Michael Banks have got nothing on those two."

"Who?" Amy squeezed her eyebrows together in confusion, and I heard Kim laugh, soft and nervous beside me.

"The kids from *Mary Poppins*. You know, Julie Andrews."

"We don't watch Disney movies."

"Oh."

I will give Amy credit for one thing: she kept her word. She told us everything.

"Their donor is a gastroenterologist. He lives in Miami and he's *gay*." She lowered her voice on *gay*, which confused me. "He's in Honduras two months a year, treating children with severe acid reflux. I guess it's common there? Anyway, he's what? Forty-five now? Something like that."

"The bank gave you all of that information?"

"More. Hang on." Amy disappeared into a room down the hall and came back holding a manila envelope stuffed with papers. She pulled a few of them out and handed them to me. "So look," she said. "You register and pick out a few profiles, and if you want to know more about one or two of them, you pay for the next level of information. I mean, they'll give you a *hand*writing analysis." Amy ticked more details off on her fingers. "A recording of his *voice*. A kindergarten picture. A detailed medical history, too, of course. On him and his immediate family."

9

"His parents?" Kim asked. I looked down at the forms, printed with all sorts of numbers and facts about her donor.

"And siblings. Grandparents, aunts and uncles."

"It's anonymous? You don't even get to know his name?"

"No way," Amy said. "They all go by numbers." She leaned over and pointed out the number printed at the top of the first form: 1316.

I looked at Kim. "This might work. I might be able to do this."

We were just so tired of searching and trying and thinking about where to get the goods. A couple of weeks before we talked to Amy, I was ready to give up. "Let's just go to Hawaii and forget about it."

"Carrie, think about the reason we're doing this."

The reason I am doing this is because I'm afraid that if I don't have a child, I'll regret it. That's the main reason. Plus, part of me thinks that once I have one child, I may want to have two or three more. I know that this is the kind of logic that most people would tell me to avoid if I ever said it out loud to anyone besides Kim, who is doing this because she wants me to have whatever I want, and I want to have a child while I still can. I'm thirty-nine. This is the absolute last minute.

Kim bought us a new house for the baby. The one she lived in when we first got together six years ago was drafty and the doors would swell in the summer humidity and stick shut. In the winter they fell open no matter how hard I pushed them into the frame. The house we live in now is in a better neighborhood near the public library and a little park and the kitchen has a stainless Sub-Zero. That refrigerator makes me feel rich. Before we moved in, I painted the bedroom next to the master a soft yellow and bought a rocking chair.

Kim also bought a new Subaru wagon for me, so that can I drive the baby from the brand new house to the doctor and the grocery and later to the neat, serious Montessori school we've picked out for the little girl or boy the baby will eventually become.

These investments made me feel a little pressured, of course. Picking out new stuff and signing papers felt so good, but I was having second thoughts about backing it all up with action. Part of what was bugging me was the reaction I got from people when I mentioned that Kim and I wanted to start a family. I told my mother over lunch at her house one afternoon early on, while I was still high on all of the planning.

"Please don't do that. I don't think you're ready for everything that comes along with that." She dragged a piece of roast chicken to the side of her plate with her fork and began dicing it into tiny pieces, which I knew from experience meant that she was getting anxious and that the afternoon would probably end in a round of hearty door slamming.

"Mom. I'm almost forty now. How much more ready am I going to get?"

"Single motherhood is difficult. I don't want you to struggle. I don't want you to get stuck in something you don't like."

"I want to have a baby, not lease a Jeep. Don't you want another grandchild?" My older brother has three boys.

"I suppose. Look, don't overreact, please. I'm thinking of you."

"And you know that I am not single." I forked up a mouthful of tomato salad and concentrated on chewing it fifty times.

"That might not last. If you add a child to that equation, you could have a lawsuit on your hands if the relationship ends, and that would really complicate your problems." I hadn't considered either of those things, ever, and it pissed me off.

"Who reacts this way? Something is wrong with you."
I laid my fork and knife across the untouched rice and gravy
on my plate and pushed back my chair.

"Something is wrong with everyone, sweetheart," she
called after me as I walked out the door.

I cried all the way home, and Kim made me a cup of
peppermint tea and told me to forget about what my mother
said. "Ignore her. I promise not to sue you over the baby,"
she said.

"Ditto."

Kim was the one who brought up using an
anonymous donor. I was against the idea at first because who
knows who those guys are? I imagined that we would
accidentally pick the one sociopath who managed to trick
their way through every one of the interview questions even
the most reputable bank would ask; a beautiful brain surgeon
with an impeccable medical history and a soul of utter evil. I
was terrified that the baby would arrive packing a strand of
defective, murder-y DNA and permanently ruin our lives
before it was old enough to chew steak.

"That wouldn't happen, Carrie. When have you
heard of something like that happening?"

"Well, it wouldn't be on the news."

"Everything is on the news. Look at it this way: we
can pick someone who doesn't have all of our hang-ups,
babe. We can control some of the hang-ups the kid may
have." This softened me. I realized that we could pick a
clean-living math whiz and possibly save the baby a lot of
grief. I could balance my chunky thigh genes with better ones,
like from a naturally thin vegetarian distance runner.

"I'll think about it."

Meantime, I kept taking the prenatal vitamins and
made sure I wasn't eating anything with artificial sweetener
and red dye. I tried to meditate every day for twenty minutes
and avoid thinking about the article I read on the *New York
Times* website about all of the problems that children with
mothers over forty are bound to have. Chromosome disasters

and severe anxiety and vicious allergies. The worst. I don't want to fool with any of that. I focused on telling myself that the baby would turn out fine and that if I nursed for a year and kept going to Pilates, I could maybe still expect my abs to snap back into place.

We decided to try with Kim's brother first so that she could be in on the deal, genetically speaking. Mike lives in Galveston and we scheduled a week of vacation days around the time we knew I'd be ovulating one month and drove down and stayed at a hotel near his house and waited for him to masturbate into an empty jelly jar every afternoon. He texted Kim right before and we would get in the car and race over. Mike met us in the driveway with the jar wrapped in a scarf that I jammed under my sweater into my armpit to keep the contents warm. Mike had decided to keep his wife in the dark, so all the action had to happen before she got home from work at five-thirty.

I had imagined that the insemination would be easy. We don't need a doctor for that, I thought. Get an oral syringe from the drugstore, load it up and fire away. The gay pregnancy book I bought said that the trick is to have an orgasm right after so that your uterus will contract and suck all of the swimmers up and then get a bunch of pillows under your hips so that gravity doesn't ruin everything. Of course, the first time we tried to do it we got in a fight before the vibrator was even turned up full speed.

"Hurry up with that, please."

"If you're tense, it's not gonna happen." Kim laid down beside me and put the vibrator between my legs and started kissing my neck. We were both getting into it when she swung her leg over me and I freaked out.

"Watch it, man! You can't jostle that stuff around. We're only going to be here for two more days. Two more tries." Kim moved off me and I put my hand over hers on the vibrator. I closed my eyes and thought about getting it on with Kathleen Hanna until I finally came, and then I scooted around and put my feet up on the headboard and we listened to "All Things Considered" on my phone for an hour.

Nothing happened with Mike's stuff, and in a way, I was relieved. He's fifteen years younger than Kim, and they don't have a close relationship. This was one of the things she emphasized to me, besides their mutual DNA. "He won't be around day-to-day, so it's perfect. We've never had much in common, anyway."

"Yeah, but you will now. You'll have something huge in common and a reason for him to come around." Kim made an "oh, I hadn't thought of that" face. It also sort of depressed me that we were trying to get pregnant in a Holiday Inn Express in Galveston. I had brought some candles and our pillows from home, but the polyester bedspread and the curtains that didn't close all the way and the rotten coffee made the whole thing feel like a business trip.

On the six-hour drive home we tried to think of anyone else we could ask and we realized that we didn't know many men and that the ones we did know wouldn't fit the bill.

"I could ask Gibbs. He's bright and he has a sharp sense of humor. He swims a mile every day."

"Kim. Gibbs is your assistant. Gibbs is a thirty-five year old man and he is still someone's assistant."

"He's working on his real estate license. Plus, that's really sexist. I'm surprised at you." Her tone let me know that she was disappointed, not surprised. I'm used to that kind of scolding. Kim is a people person. Kim is a *believer*. Her optimism is one of the reasons I love her, even though this kind of believing gets on my nerves. I am risk averse, and people are risky. Kim has a great big sugar bowl beating in her chest, and I have an old jar of cocktail olives sloshing around in mine.

"Firm no to Gibbs."

Amy kept us on her couch for three hours that afternoon, talking about follicle stimulators and basal thermometers, cervical mucus and trans-vaginal ultrasounds.

14

She explained how long it takes for a third-degree tear to heal and the importance of asking for an epidural early. "Forget the Lamaze thing. The shot makes your legs all loosey-goosey and then the baby is out before you know it. You get to have some good memories of the birth that way."

"I want that," I said. "I want good memories." I was starting to feel tired from all of the talking and nodding and the lukewarm chardonnay Amy kept pouring. "So, if you carried the babies, who did the deal?" I asked. "Sally? Or was that," I threw a fresh set of air quotes, 'too much,' too?" Amy paused, her glass in midair on the way to her mouth.

Kim cleared her throat. "She means the insemination."

"Right. Thanks, babe." I patted Kim's knee.

"Oh. Oh no, the doctor does that in the office. That's the only way to make sure everything gets connected." Amy paused and twirled an index finger in the air above her wine glass. "They put it directly into the uterus, and it gets really close to the egg. It's not cheap, you know. I'm about to order what's left of our donor's sperm with my Christmas bonus, and the bank will store it until I get ready to use it. I don't want to start all over if I decide to have number three someday."

"I can imagine," I said. "So, when you're ready to inseminate, you bring the uh, the stuff to the doctor's office?"

"The sperm." Amy said the word like I was slow, but I didn't care. I think it sounds gross. "No, your Ob-Gyn will get it for you and keep it at the office until it's time. A couple of days before our first attempt, I just called and asked the nurse to have one of the vials delivered from our storage at the bank."

Kim finally jumped in the game. "There are a lot of those, right? Sperm banks? I've started looking into it—"

"We used West Coast Cryogenics."

We thanked Amy for the wine and the conversation and said goodbye to the baby angels. As soon as we got home, Kim and I went directly to West Coast Cryogenics' website and began looking at donor profiles. The website gives you a bunch of options for picking out the perfect guy to help you make a baby. Hair color and texture. Eye color. Ethnicity. Religious preference. Level of education and areas of study. We sat and put together combinations of heights and hair color and degrees and backgrounds for an hour or so.

"Frankendaddy," I said. "This feels very 'bony-finger-of-God' to me."

"Come on, some of these guys sound great." There were plenty of attractive profiles. Each combination we typed in yielded a couple of possibilities, boxes with a man's head in silhouette. We clicked the "learn more" tab under about dozen of the ones we liked best and skimmed the paragraph of details that appeared, searching for a connection. "This one has an MFA in playwriting and a law degree. And he's 6'2." Kim said. She wanted the donor to be tall.

"Right. They're all multi-degreed athletic natural leaders who love their mothers and feel strongly committed to social justice. They're all *such* great guys. Why are they doing this? Who *are* these men?" My blood sugar was low from all of the white wine I'd had at Amy's and I was starting to get irritated. "I mean, when is the last time you even thought of the baby? I used to think about who the baby would be all the time, and now all I can think of his who the father of the baby will be."

"Donor. He's the donor and we're the parents."

"We will be the parents, you mean. If we can figure this out."

"Yes, we will be."

I saw Amy at Whole Foods a couple of weeks later, on a rainy Tuesday morning. There is something serene about that place on weekday mornings. At first I thought it was the scarcity of people in the aisles, the strange emptiness, but I noticed recently that there is a specific aroma, something earthy and sweet like freshly baked bread mixed with peppermint and pine in the air that is really soothing. I have a feeling that it's yoga studio incense residue clinging to all the Lululemon and diamonds walking around. I see the same five or six unbelievably toned blondes there at the same time every week. We silently nod at each other at the salad bar. I told a friend about this routine one Friday night over drinks and she asked me how it felt to have so much free time during the week. I felt like a spoiled jerk all of a sudden, and made up a story about wishing I had high-dollar job to go to every day. She said she'd trade places with me in a heartbeat, and I changed the subject.

Amy was in front of the dairy case with one of the twins. I tried to turn around and act interested in a display of organic popcorn before she could see me, but it was too late. She waved me over. I said hello to Amy and the little girl, who was holding a container of yogurt and a banana. "I'm thinking about making stuffed peppers tonight," I said, glancing at the cart I'd left in front of the popcorn. "It's an all-afternoon affair, but Kim loves them."

"Well, isn't she lucky. We're just getting some lunch. Mary Lucy had a doctor's appointment, and it looks like we need to keep an eye on our weight," she said in a singsong voice. Mary Lucy looked at the ground.

"I'm sure it's something she'll grow out of," I said. "Hi, Mary Lucy."

"Hi, Miss Carrie."

Amy wanted to know if Kim and I had found a donor yet. "We're working on it," I answered, forcing a big smile.

"I hope it all works out for you two. Keep me posted, okay?" She patted Mary Lucy's shoulder. "Come on, baby. I've got to get back to the office and we need to get you back to school before gym class. Carrie, is this your day off?" She eyed my outfit: Lululemon and diamonds.

"No, I work every day. At home."

"Freelance?"

"Running our household. You know, making stuffed peppers. Having a baby. Stuff like that." I've never been able to come up with a solid answer for this question. Kim said I don't have to work if I don't want to.

Amy looked at me with what I perceived as genuine wonder. "Aren't *you* the lucky one, then? What are you going to do if you can't - " She stopped herself.

"Get pregnant?"

"It's none of my business, I shouldn't have asked."

"No, it's okay. It's crossed my mind, believe me."

"So, you'll go back to work?"

"I already work. Every day. At home," I repeated. I didn't care about how that comment made me look, and it didn't seem to faze Amy, anyway. She started talking about peri-menopause, asking if I'd had my hormones checked lately. "That could gum up the works, you know. I've got some over-the-counter progesterone in here if you want some." She fished a tube of cream out of her purse and smeared some of it onto my forearm. "It's not that strong, but you might already be low, girl. How old are you again?"

"I'm twenty-nine," I lied. "Is this stuff supposed to burn?" The cream was thick and greasy, and the only way to get rid of it was to rub it off on my leggings. I wished Amy and Mary Lucy a good afternoon and went straight to the register without stopping to get the rest of my groceries. I called Kim when I got home. "I need you to get a bag of shredded cheese after work. Your horrible friend Amy made me forget to pick some up at the store. Get the organic kind."

"Oh boy. What does Amy have to do with your grocery shopping?"

"She's a disaster. I'll tell you when you get home."

Kim forgot to get the cheese, so I covered the peppers with more sauce and some breadcrumbs and shoved them under the broiler. I told her about the conversation with Amy while I sliced carrots and radishes to throw into a bowl of kale salad. "She's making one of those twins go on a diet. She's a baby! It's just baby fat."

"Didn't you tell me that the first meal your mother taught you to make was Slim-Fast and ice cubes in the blender?"

"Exactly. That's exactly what I mean."

"So this is about your stuff, not Amy's."

I jerked the pan of peppers out of the oven. "Do you want the dinner I made? Or would you rather come over here and make yourself some scrambled eggs? Because I'm about to scrape all of this into the trash. I'm not hungry anymore."

Kim took a big swallow from the glass of beer I'd poured for her when she came in from work. She looked down at her hands and adjusted her rings and her watch. This is what she does when she's on the spot and trying to think of the right thing to say. "You're going to have to lose that attitude if you want to have a baby. We can only have one baby at a time here."

This was not the right thing to say. I left the kitchen before I said something really messed up like, if you think Amy's so great, why don't you go and live at *her* fucking house? I went upstairs to my office and slammed the door, hard. I went to the cryobank's site and looked up Amy's donor. When I'd heard her say the number, I committed it to memory by singing it in my head over and over. *Thirteen-sixteen, thirteen-sixteen, thirteen-sixteen.* I knew I'd want to see what he was all about, why Amy and Sally had chosen him. *Let's see what you got, stomach doctor,* I thought to myself as I typed in the code.

I found out that night that donor 1316 is dreamy. He's six feet tall with wavy brown hair and green eyes. He is Irish, Portuguese and Scandinavian. His skin tone is medium, whatever that means, and he "keeps himself in shape with competitive cycling, swimming and yoga," according to the brief summary of his attributes provided on the bank's basic profile. "This Renaissance man balances his passion for medicine with a love of English literature and contemporary poetry. His warm charisma and brilliant sense of humor make this extrovert and admitted 'bookworm' a charming conversationalist." Alongside his profile was a little illustrated test tube blinking red, indicating that less than ten vials of donor 1316's sperm remained available. I typed in the numbers on my private, Christmas and birthday presents-only AmEx for another level of details and found out that only three vials were left.

I decided that night that I wanted 1316 to be the one. I bought the rest of the information that the bank had to offer and stayed up reading and re-reading the electronic files until daylight. He's not so exceptional, or even that unique. His childhood in a suburb of Nashville with his two younger sisters and divorced parents sounds pretty average. Everything about him, including the fact that I know that he's gay, makes 1316 feel safe and familiar. I had seen that Amy's twins resembled someone besides Amy, presumably him, and they're adorable. They hadn't been born holy terrors, and this comforted me. I waited until 7:00 a.m. to wake Kim.

"What do you think about using Amy's donor?" I sat down on the side of the bed and handed her a cup of coffee.

"Why would we do that? What's this about?" She put the cup on the bedside table and pushed herself up on an elbow. She reached for the reading glasses she'd laid on top of the novel she was reading before she went to sleep.

"You were reading *Sophie's Choice* before bed?"

"Don't change the subject, please." She put on the little half-glasses.

"I don't want you to start thinking hard yet. Just listen. Take off those Mrs. Claus glasses and listen."

"I can't see. My contacts are in the bathroom. I'm not awake yet, and you're making me think hard. This is on you."

I sighed. "Mrs. Claus, can I talk to Kim, please? Is Kim in there?"

"Enough. What's the deal with Amy's donor?"

"I remembered the number she mentioned, and I just," I looked down at my feet kicking against the bed frame, "out of curiosity, I did some research." I was starting to feel embarrassed, hearing myself explain it all out loud, "He sounds great. He sounds like a person we may want to consider."

"But there are literally thousands of others to choose from, love." She reached over and squeezed my kneecap. "Monkey bite."

I swatted her hand away. "That's right, and we don't know how that might turn out. Amy's children are great. They're turning out fine."

"Yeah, because she and Sally are raising them to be that way. I don't like this idea."

"The kids could all know each other. They would be siblings," I insisted. "Automatic sisters for the baby. It would be ideal."

"You would want Amy and Sally to know?"

"I guess." I'm still not sure why I said that. I did not want that at all.

"This contradicts everything you said about having a known donor. You said you didn't want anyone to interfere. Do you hear this contradiction? Besides, didn't Amy say that she wants to buy what's left of his sperm? She might want to try again."

"Right. She said she *might*."

Kim raised an eyebrow at me.

"Besides, you didn't mind leaving Mike's wife in the dark when he was a possibility. You seemed comfortable with that particular deception. What's the difference?"

"Amy is a person from my real life. Amy is my friend. I can't even remember Mike's wife's name."

"It's Carol, and that's not important here. Your friend is depriving those children of Julie Andrews. A child who doesn't know the words to 'Spoonful of Sugar'? It's not right. That's not childhood." I was losing ground and I knew it. I could hear myself sounding totally crazy.

"I'm sure she'll let them watch *The Sound of Music*, at least. She's a reasonable person."

21

"That's not the same and you know it. I hate this conversation. This conversation is over." I couldn't believe that Kim couldn't see the logic of 1316.

Kim has started looking for another donor in earnest. I've joined her at the computer a few nights each week since our argument, about a month now, and we've shelled out close to a grand on specific information about three other candidates who look promising: an engineer who lived on a sailboat for a year after college, an Irish-Italian attorney who plays jazz clarinet, and a choreographer who spent some time dancing with the Joffery Ballet. His celebrity look-alike, the site reports, is Mark Sanchez.

Over dinner tonight, I mentioned to Kim that I saw Dr. Smithson earlier this week, the Ob-Gyn we picked to deliver the baby. I said that I went ahead and had some blood work done, tests that indicated that my thyroid is fit and, as I suspected, my progesterone is aces. I didn't say that the doctor gave me a prescription for Clomid to start on the third day of my next period, and that when he asked me if we had decided on a donor and a date, I'd answered, "Yeah, we've found a winner. Let's start next month." I didn't mention that when the nurse asked me about having the "materials transferred" from the bank, I'd said, "It's 1316. Get all three vials."

Am I wrong for hijacking Amy's sperm? Right now, I feel nothing but excitement when I imagine the life that Kim and I can give our kid, Julie Andrews included. Kim doesn't need to know exactly where the baby came from, she's going to love it no matter what. I'm not ashamed, and one day, I'll own it all outright. I memorized the donor's number, I made the decision, and I'm the one who made the deal. I gave the nurse the number and it's my basket. I really prefer basket to "womb." It sounds cozier.

Edwin Edwards and the Lady from Dallas

Jenny was nineteen years old when she met her biological mother for the first time. It was the weekend before Mardi Gras, and the late February weather was damp and cold. Almost all of the hotel rooms in the town outside New Orleans where Jenny grew up were occupied by people who'd come to the city to catch beads and get crazy, so she had to scramble to reserve a room at a Days Inn in the suburbs a couple of miles down the interstate for the meeting. It wasn't as nice as she had imagined, but this was the only weekend that Karen, her biological mother, could drive in from Memphis to meet her before summer, and Jenny thought that there was no way that she could wait that long.

She left a box of nice candy and a glass vase full of daisies on the dresser in the room and then went to see a matinee at a dollar theatre in the neighborhood, a re-make of *Frankenstein*. This was in 1995. She couldn't concentrate on the story because she knew that by the time it was over, Karen would be in town, getting settled in that sort-of shabby hotel room. They had agreed to meet there at seven-thirty that night.

Jenny sat in the parking lot until seven thirty-five, re-reading the letter she'd gotten from Karen two weeks before. She'd opened and closed the card so many times that it didn't feel slick and crisp any more; the crease had whitened and the edges had begun to bend. She replaced the card in it's cream-colored envelope and then knocked on the hotel room door, number 135. Karen cracked it just enough to peek out and make sure that it was Jenny who was knocking. Karen opened the door and said hello like she was talking to someone she had known for a long time already. She hugged Jenny with one arm and let her go quick. There were two double beds in the room covered in shiny brown and gold polyester spreads, and Jenny sat down on the empty one. Karen had piled her stuff on the other bed: a fluffy pillow in a creased flowered

23

case, a worn, buff-colored suede shoulder bag, and a couple of magazines, Allure and Vogue. Karen had turned the covers back to expose the hotel pillows, now dented with an imprint of her shoulders, and an expensive-looking Nikon with a serious lens rested on the nightstand. The room smelled like lemon and tuberose. Karen sat on the bed next to her stuff and crossed her legs.

"You can look at me if you want to," Karen said to Jenny. Her thick auburn hair was pulled away from her face in a tight ponytail. They had the same ruddy, doughy cheeks, the same strong nose with a bump at the bridge. Karen's eyes were dark blue. Jenny's were hazel. Karen was wearing gray leggings, a baggy black cashmere sweater, and cowboy boots.

"You can look at me, too. If you want to," Jenny answered. She was wearing jeans, a red and blue flannel shirt, Doc Marten boots, thick swipes of black eyeliner, and a good amount of Ysatis perfume, which she used to disguise the odor of marijuana that clung to her clothes all the time. Her thick auburn hair was also pulled away from her face in a tight ponytail.

"You look just like Billy."

Jenny glanced at the nightstand. "Nice camera. Who's Billy?"

"Your father. Your biological father." Karen reached over and rummaged through her purse. She handed Jenny an envelope and sat down on the bed again. There were two photos in the envelope. The first one was old, bordered in white and faded. It showed a teenage boy with shoulder-length, dark brown hair, standing on a plywood riser, playing a guitar with his eyes closed. The man in the other picture looked like he was about thirty-five years old. He was wearing a button-down shirt and a black leather jacket, balancing a different guitar on his knee. His hair was long, still, past his shoulders, and he looked straight into the camera with Jenny's hazel eyes.

"Hmm. I imagined someone else." Jenny said. Karen looked surprised.

24

"I'm sorry if I'm not exactly what you expected. Or wanted to find."

Jenny looked up from the picture at Karen. "Not you. I'm not talking about you. I mean him," she held up the picture. "I expected that he would be someone else."

Karen pursed her lips in a way that made Jenny think she had expected something different, too. "Oh yeah? Like who?"

"I guess I always kind of hoped that Governor Edwards was my real dad," Jenny said.

Jenny's adoptive parents could not have children. At twenty-nine and thirty years old, most of their friends had already gotten started on what would become huge families, five or six children each, spaced just a year or two apart. When Jenny's mother decided that she couldn't take another miscarriage, they put their names on the list at Catholic Charities and waited. Eighteen months later, they got Jenny's brother Jason, and three years after that, Jenny. Jason was their father's child, and Jenny belonged to their mother. When their parents split, Jason was eight and Jenny was five. Jenny's mother wanted to go to graduate school, so she moved to a town an hour away and took Jenny. Jason and Jenny saw each other on holidays and for a few minutes every two weeks at the custody trade-off spot, the parking lot of a 7-11 in a town exactly halfway between their new homes.

Jason went crazy when he found out he was adopted. He was eleven. An older cousin said that he and his sister were "little bastards" and asked him, "Do you know what that means?" He broke their dad's nose with a t-ball trophy when he told him the truth, and then called their mom and tried to get her to say that it was a lie, but she wouldn't. Years later, he told Jenny that he had begged their mom to let him talk to Jenny that night, but she said no, and that he hadn't ever forgiven her for it. Their mother was afraid that Jason would tell Jenny, too, and she wanted to do that herself.

She waited until Jenny was in the bathtub, that same night. They had had some other serious talks there, including a tear-filled demystification of Santa Clause the year before. She let Jenny shake as much Mr. Bubble into the water as she wanted for a change, and put a little glass of chocolate milk on the side of the tub. As she scooped water into a plastic cup and poured it over Jenny's shoulders and back, her mother explained that when some babies are born, they aren't with the right parents, so different ones have to come and get them. She said that this is how Jason and Jenny were chosen, and that it made them something special.

"We're not your real babies?" Jenny asked.

"Yes, you are. Yes and no."

"Who are our other parents?"

"I don't know who they are. When you're grown you can find out if you want."

"Who do you *think* it is?"

"I don't know, Jenny. Who do *you* think it is?" She lifted Jenny out of the bathtub and wrapped her in a towel in her arms.

Jenny had called Karen for the first time ten days before they met. She spent hours rehearsing beforehand so that she could make sure that when they spoke, Karen got the impression that she was artistic and independent. She planned to prove this by saying that she was taking a year off from school to research Cajun folklore in the Atchafalaya Basin. Karen's voice caught Jenny off guard when she answered the phone. It was tentative, and she was expecting it to be confident and warm. Jenny wanted Karen's voice to crack and then break into a sob. She wanted Karen to say "I have waited so long for this to happen." Something like that.

Instead, they made small talk about their day for a few minutes, and Karen asked Jenny one question about herself. "So, what did you have for dinner?"

"Spaghetti," Jenny answered, stretching the phone cord straight and then letting it spring back into a coil over and over again. "My mom made spaghetti." Jenny tensed, wondering how Karen felt about her calling her mother "mom." Would Karen expect Jenny to call *her* that? Karen had eaten sushi for dinner. Wasabi tobiko, to be exact, with her boyfriend, who she lived with in Memphis. "He's not your father," she said to Jenny. "He owns a record store. All vinyl." She told Jenny that her favorite place to vacation was Oaxaca and that she traveled for two years after college, going to concerts and dropping acid with the record store guy.

Then it was Jenny's turn to talk, and she blanked. She forgot to tell Karen that she wanted to live on a houseboat and then maybe become a midwife or start a theatre company. She told Karen that she failed all of her classes at LSU in the fall and moved back home with her mother. She told her that she was trying to quit smoking cigarettes, but not pot, and that her favorite movie was *Hannah and Her Sisters.*

Karen proposed the meeting, saying that she wanted to talk about the details of Jenny's birth in person. Their first conversation lasted twenty-three minutes.

In the hotel room after the pictures, Karen let Jenny ask her questions. She told Jenny everything she wanted to know, and some things she didn't want to know ended up mixed into the conversation, too.

Jenny's father was a guy Karen dated in high school. He was a senior, and she was a freshman. "My parents hated him. He was way too old for me and he never wore shoes. I mean, I lost my virginity, and then there was you. It happened at a party over Memorial Day weekend. My parents were out of town."

"So, you were drinking?"

"Probably. It was a long, long time ago. I guess we were drinking."

"What did your parents say when you told them?"

"They were appalled. They wanted to take me to get it taken care of, but it was too late."

"Did they decide to put me up for adoption, then?"

"We all did. I wanted to go to college and travel. Plus, I was way too young to raise you, and Billy and I didn't last through the summer. His parents made him get a job on a rig offshore when he graduated."

"Made him?"

"Pretty much."

Karen said all of these things casually, as if Jenny was one of her girlfriends. Jenny concentrated on memorizing the details of what Karen was saying. When Karen finished talking, Jenny stood up to leave. "I'll come by and get you at ten-thirty tomorrow morning. It'll take a while to get to my mom's. The parades. She's excited about meeting you." Karen gave Jenny another side-hug, patting her back a little too hard. "Easy, killer," Jenny laughed, and left the hotel room.

Jenny pulled out of the hotel parking lot and took a back road along the bayou to Jason's house. He knew she was meeting Karen that night. Jenny had called Jason first when the social worker from Catholic Charities let her know that she had found Karen.

"It was one of the easiest contacts I have ever made," the woman had said. "Her parents have had the same phone number since nineteen-seventy. I said that I was a friend from high school, and the woman who answered just gave up her number." Jenny thought she sounded pretty pleased with herself.

Jason was watching television with his girlfriend, Ashley, when she arrived. Ashley was five months pregnant, and while Jason went to the kitchen and fixed them all big bowls of pecan pie and vanilla ice cream, she showed Jenny a couple of sonogram images of the daughter they would have in the spring. Jenny and Jason took their bowls into the spare bedroom he used for a study and closed the door. Jenny sat at

28

his desk and begin to methodically eat the pie, dragging each bite through the melting ice cream first. Jason turned the stereo on before he sat down so that Ashley couldn't hear what they were saying.

"What was it like with Karen?" Jason asked.

"I don't know yet. We look alike, kind of. It was like nothing." Jenny shrugged, looking up at the pictures of David Bowie taped to the wall over Jason's desk. The Thin White Duke. She felt the edges of a lump forming in her throat, fighting against a wad of pecans and syrup.

"Jenny. You didn't go looking for nothing. Say more about Karen." She could tell that Jason was practicing therapy on her. He wanted to be a shrink. "Where is that letter?"

"In my car. I put it away." He was talking about the letter Jenny received from Karen through the adoption agency two weeks before.

"Let's go."

In the driveway, Jenny took the pictures of Billy Shields and a cream colored envelope out of her car's glove compartment. The card inside had a rendering of "Portrait of Madame X" by John Singer Sargent on its cover. Jason and Jenny lighted cigarettes and he read the letter out loud.

Hello Jennifer-

My name is Karen Williams. I have written and re-written this letter in my mind a hundred times. I want you to know that I have spent many hours thinking, and wondering, about you.

I live in Memphis, but I grew up in Baton Rouge. My parents still live there, and I visit them a few times a year. I am working in finance here, but plan to return to school within the next year or so to study art history. That is something I promised myself I would do before I turn 40, so I don't have much time, ha ha!

Jennifer, I would like to get to know you. I know that you must have many questions for me. I hope that I can answer them all for you, and I look forward to meeting you in person soon, if you wish.

Take care-
Karen

Written below Karen's phone number at the bottom of the letter: *Give me a call when you are ready. After 7 is fine.*

Jenny had been carrying the letter in her coat pocket, constantly checking and re-checking to make sure it was still there. Karen had tucked a picture of herself inside the letter. In it, she was wearing a pair of striped overalls, smiling directly at the camera over a flat, white-iced cake. Smoke from a cluster of pink candles, recently extinguished, wreathed her face, and on the back, "Birthday '93" was written in blue ink.

"Is this the woman that you met tonight?" Jason shook the card and photo, one in each hand. "Jenny, this is what you say you've been dying for. I was expecting you to be excited. What's wrong with her? Was she ugly to you?"

"No, she was nice. She was fine. Stop pushing me, Jason. She's my person. When are you going to find out about your people?"

"Maybe never. I don't want to know."

"That's a lie. You're using me and Karen for practice, and you know that you are lying. You know you're afraid."

Jason blew a long plume of cigarette smoke in the direction of his sister's face, a sort of private shorthand between the two of them, a nonverbal way of saying, "fuck you." Jenny snatched the cigarette from his fingers and threw it on the ground. "I would only want to know for the baby," Jason said. "Ashley's bugging me about the medical history."

"Lies." Jenny knew she was being too hard on him. "She gave me some pictures of my father." She handed the pictures to Jason. "Billy Shields."

He laid the pictures of my Billy next to the picture of Karen on the hood of Jenny's car and examined them, looking up at Jenny, and then back at the pictures.

"Too bad about the gov."

"I know. She didn't get it."

30

"Aw, Jen you told her?" Jason shoved her shoulder and she flicked the butt of her cigarette into the street. "Now she's gonna think you're crazy."

"Who cares? She's meeting mom bright and early. Please show up over there around lunchtime, okay? I don't want to be alone with them. "

Jason put his hands on her shoulders and looked into her eyes. Jenny looked down at the ground, at his red Converse. At her boots. "Say that you're disappointed, sister. It's okay to be let down."

"I'm not, bub. She's okay. She has this awesome camera."

"Did she take a picture of you?"

"No."

Jenny never talked to her mom about all of her fantasy "real" mothers because she don't want to hurt her feelings, but she thought about this all the time. Jenny was a thumb sucker. She sucked her thumb until she was twelve years old, and then she started smoking cigarettes. Her parents took her to a pediatrician and then to a therapist who explained that these behaviors were probably an oral fixation caused by the fact that she hadn't been breast fed. Jenny thought that was stupid. Jason never sucked his thumb. She tried to explain that when she was sucking her thumb, she felt a soft click in the back of her brain, and the click would turn into a daydream. Her daydream list of "real" mothers was long. If she saw a pretty lady in the grocery store, or if her teacher was really sweet, she would think, "Is it you?" When her mother pissed her off by grounding her or misunderstanding her, she comforted herself with these fantasies.

Famous people. For a while it was Dolly Parton, who was eventually replaced by Stevie Nicks from the cover of *Belladonna*, and then the actress who played Sue Ellen Ewing on *Dallas*, an ironic choice, since her mother actually

31

subscribed to a similar aesthetic: big jewelry, fur coats and dramatic eye makeup.

Jenny never wondered about her biological father, ever. Instead of constructing an elaborate fantasy about who he was, she found a guy to hold his place, and she left him there until pictures of Billy Shields arrived.

Jenny is eight years old. She is fitting pieces into a corner of a teddy bear puzzle on the coffee table in the living room of the house where she lives with her mother, who is sitting on the couch in a silky pink kimono, drinking a glass of white wine. The news comes on. "That womanizer," she mutters. "Him and his *pupuns*."

She is talking about Edwin Edwards, the governor of Louisiana, who is on TV cutting a ribbon with an enormous pair of scissors in front of a renovated wing of the state capitol building in Baton Rouge.

"What's a womanizer?"

"Nothing baby, he just likes to take ladies out to eat."

Jenny turns back toward the screen. The ribbon's ends lie in puddles on the ground, and the man is shaking hands in a crowd gathered around him. The camera pulls in close as he brushes a wing of silvery bangs off his tan forehead. He laughs at something one of the women in the crowd has leaned in to say, shifting a piece of chewing gum in his mouth in a flash of gleaming white teeth. He straightens up and throws his chest out, pulling down on the lapels of his pinstriped suit jacket, and then turns and struts through the capitol doors, flanked by a pair of state troopers.

The man on television is handsome, and Jenny thinks that taking a lady out to eat is a really nice thing to do. She is too little to know the meaning of words like corruption, fraud or infidelity. This moment is her introduction to the phenomena of personal charisma. What she sees is that everyone in the crowd is laughing, and loving him.

"That's my daddy! That's my real daddy." She jumps up and points at the screen. The spell is broken. A commercial for Jif peanut butter.

"Your dad's a policeman in Shreveport, not Baton Rouge, monkey. Go put on your pajamas. That's enough excitement for tonight."

"No, the ribbon man! That womanizer is my real daddy." She sweeps the puzzle onto the carpet. Pieces of cardboard bounce off the bricks of the fireplace.

Jenny's mom gets up and marches her by the shoulders upstairs to her room. She pulls a nightgown over Jenny's head while her daughter wails into her hands, furious. She spoons up a big dose of cherry Tylenol to settle Jenny, and then they read part of *Where the Sidewalk Ends* together. "They can be whoever you want for now, babe. It can be anyone." Her mother turns off the light.

Jenny saw her mother asleep on the couch when she got home from Jason's. She woke up when she heard Jenny rattling the foil on a pan of brownies in the kitchen.

"Jen?"

"Hey Mom." Jenny didn't want to talk to her mom about Karen or Billy. "See you in the morning." She ran upstairs to her room before her mother could stop her, kicked off her jeans and got under the covers, still in her flannel and eyeliner. She thought about what it might be like to meet Billy, who probably lived in a regular brick ranch instead of a mansion in downtown Baton Rouge. She broke up the brownies and shoved the pieces into her mouth while she read Karen's letter again.

Snapdragon

Elise convinced Jody that they wanted two dollar martinis more than they wanted dinner, so they walked five blocks to a bar one evening after figure drawing class, leaving their cars in the parking lot of the university art department. Jody was the reason Elise had started thinking she was a lesbian. Jody was the most talented student in the class, and Elise modeled nude for twelve dollars cash an hour. Jody's sketches began to focus solely on the plane of Elise's inner thigh and the crease where her collarbone joined her neck, and when Elise noticed, she wrote her phone number across the likeness of her own ribcage while Jody was outside smoking. The other students, bashful at working with their first live model, stuck to penciling out her form with rote, literal fidelity to her anatomy, with the exception of one young woman who concentrated her efforts on rendering the cellulite that coated Elise's buttocks and upper thighs with detached precision. The instructor declared her expression of the Keratosis Pilaris on Elise's haunches "masterful." This burned Jody up. She seduced Elise after class that evening. Elise slept at her apartment that night and never went home. They'd been together this way for ten months.

The bar they stopped at was called the Sidecar, and it was packed. Women in pencil skirts and heels, businessmen in shirtsleeves, a swarm of collegiate types. Elise had gone out looking like hell, her dirty hair scraped into a bun, no makeup and a cheap flowered sundress with rubber flip flops. "Hey Nineteen" was playing on the jukebox, and Elise and Jody downed their first drinks fast and kissed a few times, standing up between occupied stools. Jody ordered two more over Elise's shoulder and went to the ladies' room. At the other end of the bar, Kevin Baudoin was letting a woman whose hair he'd just cut into a deliberately messy shag buy him drinks. Every now and then, he reached over and separated her bangs into even messier pieces, or stuck his clawed hand in at the nape of her neck and shook her ashy layers into

34

chaos. Elise watched the lady arch her back and giggle. She liked Kevin's attention.

Kevin looked okay. Elise recognized him from the time she'd dropped her mother off at his salon after she'd had lipo and couldn't drive. He had called her mother "dollface," which had embarrassed Elise. He was dressed the way she remembered that night, in tight, straight-leg Levi's and a faded black V-neck. Black Chucks. "He thinks he's Mick Jagger," her mother had said. Kevin was skinny and tan, with long arms and legs. Elise imagined he was something like fifty-five years old. She stared at him working his client, pouring some of whatever was in his rocks glass over into hers. Jody came back and put her arms around Elise's waist from behind, "I need to leave for work soon," she whispered. Jody paid for school by working the night shift at a drive through daiquiri shop near the north gate of LSU.

Elise wanted to stay and drink. She had enough cash to buy three more martinis and still pitch in for half of the groceries that week. "Why don't you call me on your break?" she said to Jody. "I can walk back to my car, no problem." Jody left and two drinks later the lady Kevin was flattering left and the bar started to empty out a little bit. "Tusk" came on. Elise walked outside to smoke a cigarette and Kevin followed. "Drop that hair, I want to see what you've got," he teased, offering her a light.

"It's filthy, I need a color," she pointed her lighted cigarette in the direction of her crown, exhaling.

Kevin reached over and removed the number two pencil Elise had stabbed into her bun to hold it in place. "You're right," he said, wincing in a fake way that bugged Elise, "it's bad. Let me fix you up." He pulled a business card out of his back pocket and handed it over. Elise patted the place where her sundress flared over her hips.

"No pockets, brah. Sorry," she laughed. She wanted him to realize she wasn't sorry. Elise and Kevin went back inside the bar and kept drinking martinis and talking. When Elise ran out of money, Kevin ordered them a couple of draft beers and told the bartender to put them on his tab. He told Elise that he had seen her walk in with Jody.

"So, she's the boy and you're the girl?" Jody wore her blue-black hair in a quiff, and she dressed like Kevin, androgynous, in tight, dark clothes.

Ordinarily, a question like this activated a tape in Elise's head of the theoretical noise she had learned in her women's studies classes, but Elise was drunk and feeling generous. "Is that where your mind wants to go right now?" she tapped her temple. "Is that your big fantasy about me and my girl?"

Kevin put his hand on her thigh, "I like it well enough for now. Guys and girls. Works for me."

"We just got together, anyway. She thinks I drink too much to fall in love with."

"She said that?"

"I can just tell."

"You don't need that," he was rubbing her leg, squeezing her kneecap, "you're so pretty, honey. You look so good." Kevin dove at her neck and she let him. He paid the tab and acted like he wanted to walk Elise to her car. "Why don't I drive you home instead?" he suggested. Kevin said he wanted to go by his shop first and pick up some cash to deposit the next day. He said he didn't like to leave it in the register overnight. "Let me show you where my place is. Come in on Saturday and I'll make you perfect again," he said, freeing her hair again and twisting the length of it like a jump rope.

By the time they got to the narrow storefront that Kevin rented in downtown Baton Rouge, Elise needed to go inside and pee. "That draft put me over," she laughed. "I usually stick to clear liquor."

The place was meant to look like an Asian fantasy, with big garnet colored cushions piled on black lacquer futon frames and rice paper screens partitioning off the area between the shampoo bowl and the chair where Kevin cut hair. The salon smelled of sulfur and expensive shampoo, like rotten eggs mixed with tea rose and jasmine. Kevin smelled like sandalwood, Elise discovered, when he leaned her back in the shampoo bowl and began kissing her neck again. "Are you going to cut my hair?" she asked, and closed her eyes. Kevin's kisses felt good, and she thought he was probably right. She didn't need Jody's criticism. She liked drinking. She was having fun.

"Maybe later," he answered, and reached under her skirt.

The sex was a disaster. Elise couldn't focus the way you need to in a one night stand, that mixture of, "holy shit, this is happening," and, "is the rubber still on? Wait...okay, yeah: do that. No, *that*." She was too wasted to really get wet, so Kevin's half-hard dick sort of bounced out a few times before she finally pushed him back and gave up an unenthusiastic blowjob. He offered her some cocaine, snorting a fat rail off a hand mirror balanced on the shampoo shelf, but she was done. There were a bunch of cans of Sprite in a little fridge next to the bathroom, and she downed half a cold soda before making a bed out of a pile of black nylon smocks she found hanging on the back of the door. The last thing she remembered was seeing Kevin sitting on the toilet lid above her, rolling a joint. "I just need to close my eyes for a minute," she said.

"Okay, dollface, let's get you moving," Kevin set a Styrofoam cup of coffee in front of Elise's face and hauled her up to sitting by her upper arm, and then he was squatting next to her with his arms wrapped around her ribcage, patting her back. She swallowed what was left in the soda can on the floor next to her and lunged for the toilet. Kevin rubbed her back while she retched. "I called you a cab, baby. My first client will be here in twenty minutes."

"Get away from me, man." As she pushed him off, Elise could see that Kevin's hair was damp and he was wearing a different t-shirt, a white one. His sandalwood smell was stronger, with cigarette smoke underneath. He had on a pair of frameless half-glasses, which made him look older. He looked his age to Elise just then, her mother and father's age, pushing sixty. "Did you leave me here last night?"

"You were out. All the way out."

"Where's my stuff?" She was naked except for her bra and the smock that lay bunched over her legs.

"Where you left it. Come on, I'll help you."

"Give me that." Elise nodded at Kevin's coffee.

Her dress was wedged in the hinge of the chair in front of the shampoo bowl. As she jerked it free, she noticed a pack of cigarettes lying on Kevin's station next to a jar full of black plastic combs submerged in Barbicide. A twenty was folded between the cellophane and the paper of the pack. Elise stuck the pack in her bra.

Kevin gave her a fresh coffee and money for the cab and he kissed her forehead at the door. She asked the driver to take her to her parents' house. She didn't want to explain where she'd been to Jody, and she had left her keys and cigarettes at the Sidecar anyway. Her parents kept a spare front door key under a ceramic turtle next their garage. Elise stripped off her sundress and panties in the kitchen, and then removed the cigarette pack from her bra. The clock on the microwave read nine-thirty. She took a carton of orange juice into the backyard and launched herself into the middle of her parents' swimming pool on a plastic raft. In the hot light, Elise inspected her body. The chlorinated water burned at something on her hip, a raw archipelago of purpling ovals with a crust of drying blood where an incisor had broken the skin.

Jody was pissed when Elise finally turned up at their apartment.

"I thought something fucking horrible had happened to you. You can't just not come home."

"I did go home, though. I went to my parents' house last night. I wanted to sleep alone. We're not girlfriends, remember? I mean, my stuff is here," Elise swept her arm in

38

the direction of an overstuffed laundry basket filled with folded clean clothes, "but this is your place. You don't even know what you're doing with me."

"You could have called."

"My phone is dead."

"Your parents don't have a phone."

"I was tired, lay off!"

Elise took a bath and then she and Jody had makeup sex. Afterward, Jody told Elise that she would make space for her in the closet and on the shelves in the bathroom, and that she wanted her to feel like the apartment was her place, too. They could take things slowly.

"Let's just see where this goes," she said, pulling Elise closer, kissing the top of her head.

Elise wanted Jody to want her. She had been living with Jody, but in a half-hearted way, using the shampoo she found in the shower instead of getting a bottle of the kind she liked, asking Jody for permission to open a cabinet or take a book off a shelf. She liked the way Jody looked, all sinew and bone, covered in tattoos. The knuckles of her right hand read: blasé; her left: blasé. She liked sleeping with Jody. She liked that Jody was a good artist. She had a lot of ideas about Jody, and she liked almost all of them.

"Okay," she said. "We'll see."

The next morning, Jody found the bruises on Elise's hip, along with a couple of livid hickeys that had surfaced on Elise's ribcage. "Are you going to keep seeing him?" Jody asked. She had listened to Elise explain the night with Kevin with a look of complete equanimity.

Elise winced. "Of course not. I never want to see him again. We are together," she pointed a forefinger at Jody's chest and back at her own, "remember?"

Jody shrugged her off and got dressed for class. "Do you want coffee?" she called from the kitchen. "We have green tea."

Elise threw the covers off and went to the bathroom to pee. She eased open the medicine cabinet. Clear nail polish.

Eyeliner pencils. Floss. Eye drops. Bingo: Elise palmed the bottle of Xanax and flushed the toilet. "Diet Coke," she answered, and slipped a powdery pill onto her tongue. She chased it with a scoop of water from the tap, and then met Jody in the tiny kitchen. "I need cigs. See you at school."

She drove to the Circle K near campus and bought smokes and a pint of Crown. She twisted through the bottle's plastic seal as she started the car. She figured she had about twenty-seven minutes to drink, drive, park, change, and get in place for class. She pulled hard on the bottle twice and sipped on the Diet Coke as she navigated afternoon traffic. In the art department parking lot, she added a healthy slug of whiskey to the rest of the soda and took two more Xanax, then hurried into the bathroom and out of her cutoffs. Naked, she wobbled a little on one foot getting into the old button-down of her father's she wore instead of a robe. Just get on the platform and go to sleep, she told herself.

The students wanted gestures, though. Forty-five minutes of natural poses, three minutes per pose. The instructor handed Elise a broom handle and set a wooden box on the riser where she usually curled herself into approximations of yoga twists or laid across an aged, peeling beanbag that belonged to the department. She decided to begin with the handle, staking it on the plywood and leaning away and to the right with her arms outstretched. Then she leaned left. This made her head spin, so she rested a foot on the box and held the handle aloft like a sword. She connected it to an invisible baseball at the level of her chest. She abandoned it and kneeled on the box, her fingers gripping the sides. A warped, wah-wah sound filled her ears and she passed out. She fell off the step and hit the ground face first.

The ambulance the instructor called took her to a charity hospital that kept her in detox for exactly seventy-two hours. The nurse who started her IV asked if she thought she might be pregnant.

"Lady, I'm gay," she mumbled.

Jody yelled at her for embarrassing herself in front of the class and making Jody look like an ass. "They all think I'm on whatever you're on, probably."

"I'm not on anything. I was just a little drunk. I had a drink before class."

"When? I saw you less than an hour before class started and you were fine."

Elise learned from the instructor of the drawing class that Jody had tried to convince him to let her take Elise home, that she was just exhausted and probably had low blood sugar. "You were in bad shape," he told Elise. "I can't take a chance like that with a studio full of students. Come and see me when you get well."

"I'm well now," she begged. "Please, just let me finish the semester."

No dice. "Sweetheart, you've got bruises all over." He took her arm and gently held it up, as if she hadn't yet seen the black and purple marks there. "I can see that black eye through your makeup. Get some help and then come and see me."

Jody told Elise not to worry about working, to focus on taking care of herself. She wanted Elise to start going to meetings. "I'll go with you." The recovery groups met at about a million places in Baton Rouge, but Elise and Jody mostly went to the ones behind a Domino's Pizza near their apartment in an aluminum sided building the size of a two-car garage. It had a large, awkward front porch that someone had hammered on for what looked like the sole purpose of accommodating the many smokers at each meeting, including Elise and Jody.

"I used to wonder what this place was all the time," Elise said. "I would drive by and see people out here smoking and talking at all hours of the day and night and think, who *are* you all? Why aren't you at work? Know what I mean?"

"That's like, your tenth cigarette today. I thought you were going to slow down," Jody answered.

41

The interior of the meeting place was jammed with the remnants of peoples' sad living rooms, tons of sprung recliners and smoke saturated couches whose crumbly foam cushions depicted scenes of the old West: orange and brown covered wagons, muscular ponies. A lacquered wagon wheel coffee table in the center of the room held a stack of books that outlined the rules everyone had to follow to stop getting loaded.

Hearing the other people in the meetings talk about the mistakes they made while they were wasted got on Elise's nerves, which still felt electrified and raw from not drinking. She'd never stopped for more than three days in a row before. Elise stayed quiet. Jody did not.

Elise learned that Jody had some pretty good stories to tell. She did not know that Jody had three older sisters, or that she had started going out to bars and partying with them when she was fourteen. She didn't know that Jody's parents had kicked her out a few years later when she came out. She learned for the first time that Jody had spent a few years dancing in New Orleans, doing speed and gaming on the rich guys who drove in for the weekend to gamble, and that she had spent a night in jail in a teddy and a pair of clear plastic heels when she got arrested for smashing another stripper in the face with a bottle of Victoria's Secret body spray.

"I thought you might freak out about some of that stuff," Jody confessed when Elise brought it up later, at home.

Elise laughed. "Do you know me at all? I like danger. It turns me on," she said, and raised an eyebrow. She was not joking. The version of Jody that lived in the stories was more closely aligned with the person she met on the first day of drawing class. Wild. She still dressed like a bum crossed with a rock star, but the real Jody was fussy about the way Elise folded towels and liked to read the recovery group's daily affirmations out loud while she ate high-fiber cereal every morning. Even Jody's artwork began to reflect the influence of what she heard in the group. She made a new painting or

42

collage for every action the book suggested they take to keep from drinking.

One of the first actions was all about believing in God, written in a really non-specific way so as not to chase off the sensitive ones who blamed Him for their hard times. The book laid off using the G-word, but the name they used sounded too controlling to Elise, so she called it Greater Energy instead. She didn't have any hard feelings for the God in the religion she had been served since childhood, and she liked its plaster statues and pictures of dramatically exposed flaming hearts and pregnant teenage queens. She kept some good-luck holy cards jammed into her car's dash, which made Jody nervous.

"How can you see the gas gauge?"

"The Virgin Mary has my back."

Jody told Elise that she didn't believe in God. "I just have a conscience," she said one night as they made dinner.

"That's your Greater Energy, then. It doesn't have to be a specific person, like a man with a white beard pointing at you with a bony finger."

"It's not one person. It's two people. Two men."

This got Elise's attention

"When I need to make a decision, I go in my head first. I've had this image of two men there for as long as I can remember. I ask them if I'm doing the right thing, and they give me the answer."

"How's that?' Elise looked away and kept her voice even so that Jody would keep talking.

"Well, my yes man is on the right side, and my no man is on the left."

"Left and right side of what? Your hands?"

"My mind. The picture in my mind." Jody's face and neck began to flush. "Look, never mind. I can't."

"No, keep going. I won't say anything else."

"Okay. So, say I ask something and the answer is yes. The man on the right will lift his face to the sky and blaze light at me. Like, he's surrounded by rays of light, and when he looks up, it's a blaze of that light. If the answer is no, the left hand guy will show up and bow his head, and the lights around him all go out. It sounds like a door slamming."

"What do they look like?"

"Yes man is wrapped in this white and gold robe and he's barefoot. He has long brown hair and white, white teeth. He's always standing in the wind, too, like his hair and his robe are always blowing back. No man is like a mummy, almost. He's covered in these raggedy bluish gray bandages, even his head. I've never seen his eyes."

"Okay, so that's Jesus, babe. Thanks for playing."

"It's not, though."

"I want that. I want people to help me make decisions."

"You need to look at the pictures in your head, then."

After that, every time she needed to make a decision, Elise tried to find an image of her Greater Energy in her head. She began with minutia. *Should I smoke this cigarette now or after I take a shower?* Darkness. *Skirt or shorts?* Nothing. Elise started telling Jody that she wanted to go to some different meetings alone, and then going over to her parents' house to swim and lay out instead. She was sick of listening to people swallow coffee and complain about their grown children who refused to speak to them. She pretended to Jody that she was still reading the book and following the actions it recommended. One night, she decided to go out to a bar downtown to watch a Cajun band and dance. Jody didn't want to go.

"Why would you put yourself in a situation to be tempted? You're doing so much better, I can really tell a difference." It was true. Elise did feel livelier, and she had gotten used to not drinking. She liked the feeling of waking up after sleeping all night long, hard.

"Nothing's going to happen. I don't even feel like drinking anymore. I'm way more into eating my feelings now, anyway," she said.

The band hadn't started when she arrived, and the first person she saw was Kevin Baudoin, talking to the bartender. She turned around and walked back to her car. She smoked a cigarette. She flipped down the visor and reapplied her lipstick. She closed her eyes. *Should I go back inside?* In her mind, a waxy green flower with teeth appeared. The teeth parted and the flower hinged open. It's deep pink interior spit out a single, fat black fly. She went back inside.

Avoiding Kevin was no problem since the dance floor in front of the stage was crammed with people. She kept him in her peripheral vision, making sure to move when he got too close to where she was dancing. She went to the bar and ordered a Coke, but the bartender set a glass of draft in front of her. He lifted his chin at the crowd behind Elise and she turned around. Kevin.

"I don't want this." She did want the beer, though. She could imagine how it tasted and how much better it would make the music sound. The flower with teeth recaptured the fly and hinged closed.

"He already paid for it."

"So? I don't want this." As she pushed the glass at him, some of the draft sloshed onto her hand, and she slurped at it without thinking. "Give me a Coke." She laid a five-dollar bill on the bar and left with her plastic cup of soda.

"My Greater Energy is a snapdragon." Jody was asleep when Elise came home and told her about the bar and Kevin. Jody sat up in bed in the dark while Elise took off her dress and boots and her makeup in the bathroom attached to their room.

"It sounds like a Venus flytrap, not a snapdragon."

"Whatever. I say snapdragon."

"You didn't drink."

"No."

"You never spoke to him."

"No."

45

"Okay. I mean, you'll have to face him sooner or later."

"Why? I told you I never want to see him again."

"You have to make it right with him, Elise. You took his money and his cigarettes, remember? You have to make an apology." Jody was big on apologies now. Elise had forgotten that she told Jody about the smokes and the twenty she'd lifted from Kevin.

Jody got out of bed and put her arms around Elise's waist, and then hooked her chin over Elise's shoulder and addressed her reflection in the bathroom mirror, "Please don't start fucking up, love. We're doing so good. Isn't this what you wanted?"

Elise leaned back into Jody. "I think so. Yes. This is what I wanted."

Jody helped her rehearse the speech she would give Kevin when she went to make the apology, and even offered to drive Elise to the salon and wait in the car while she did it.

"Say it all one more time so you'll be ready," she urged on the morning Elise was supposed to go to Kevin's shop. She didn't know that Elise had made an appointment to have her bangs cut using her initials. "E.J. Briggs," she had said when she called. "Just a trim."

She wore the same flowered sundress from the night they'd fucked, or tried to, and twisted her hair into a bun again. She stopped for a fresh pack of cigarettes to make up for the ones she stole, and attached a folded twenty with a ponytail holder. Kevin looked surprised when she walked in at ten o'clock, sharp.

"Hey, honey. What you know good?" He was sitting at his desk, examining a computer screen through his old man half glasses.

"I'm here for a haircut," she said.

"Well, let's see," he searched the screen, clicking up and down with the mouse. "I'm booked right now, but-"

"I have an appointment. E.J. Briggs. Bangs," she smoothed her fringe down over her eyebrows, "they're still a disaster."

Kevin took his time washing her hair and combing out the tangles. He offered to trim the ends, too. "No charge."

Elise checked. Open. The fly circled the pink maw. "Okay. Just a half inch or so."

He snipped her bangs precisely, his face inches from her crown. "I need to tell you something, Kevin," she said, careful not to move. "I was wrong and I need to make something right." Still open.

"Sure, baby. What's that?"

"I brought you those cigarettes. The money is for you, too. I took your cigarettes and your money the last time I was here."

"You don't have to pay me just yet. You don't have to pay me at all. I wanted to see you again." He lowered his shears and kissed her, "I told you I would make you perfect, remember?"

The fly darted between the snapdragon's teeth as it began to close. She pulled him closer by the buckle of his belt. "When is your next appointment?"

Jody wanted details when she got home from school that afternoon, "Was it okay? Did he accept your apology?"

The jaws had flown open. The fly swooped in from the left, then the right, grazing the dark interior with abandon. "Definitely," Elise said. "He was very kind about the whole thing. I told him that I was doing it as much for myself as I was for him. It was perfect."

Gulnar Means Rose

Kelly saw Bingo for the first time on Oprah. The episode was on spirituality in Hollywood, and a supermodel, famous in the early 1990's and still bronze and dewy at forty-five, was discussing her discovery of Bingo's teaching, explaining all of the ways it had changed her life. "I can't believe how much joy I have been able to manifest. I think of my interactions with others so differently now. Especially men. I compare every guy I meet to Bingo," she admitted, covering her mouth as she laughed. "He's really something special." She went on to explain her recent career revival, giving all of the credit for "the best year of my life" to Bingo, who was patched in remotely from Maui. "I'm spending the week helping fifty remarkable souls learn to manifest their dearest desires," he explained. The supermodel blew him a kiss, promising to "call you soon, my darling." Oprah thanked him for joining the conversation, and then moved on to a segment on an astrologer in New York City who had just three clients, all Academy award-winning actresses.

Kelly was home from work with the flu, and the mixture of over-the-counter remedies she had taken for her cough and fever, plus the cup of chamomile tea she'd consumed, was making her feel sleepy and sentimental. She'd been marooned on the couch all day, but her curiosity about Bingo motivated her to kick off the blankets covering her legs and find her phone. She typed his name into a search engine. The first three articles that appeared were recent, just six weeks old, and covered a tragedy that had occurred at a retreat center he owned near Sedona, Arizona. The headline of the first link read: "Fire at Guru's Luxe Hideaway Kills Three." Kelly learned that the fire had been investigated and declared an accident - candles left burning near an open window, a set of raw silk drapes. A brisk wind. Bingo was leading a workshop in San Francisco at the time, and when asked for a comment regarding the loss of three of what the Arizona Daily Sun referred to as his "followers," he said only that, "Their hunger is finally satisfied. I will miss them. My roses." She clicked another link to a page full of images of Bingo, a middle-aged white man with golden brown eyes and a square chin covered in salt and pepper stubble. His head was ringed in the same stubble, save for a gleaming bald spot at his crown. *Nothing special*, Kelly thought, and kept scrolling.

Wikipedia reported that Bingo was born Albert Michael Thompson in Shreveport, Louisiana in 1956, and currently resided in Mandeville, an affluent suburb of New Orleans. Raised by his grandmother, he claimed to have chosen the name Bingo as a tribute to the thing that made her most happy in life. "She taught me so much that prepared me to do this work," he said in an interview with *The Times-Picayune* in 1995. "She knew how to focus all of her intention, one card at a time. She was my first model of what I believe was pure Zen."

In the section marked "Personal Life," Kelly found that Albert had been married twice in his twenties and taken the name Bingo, along with a vow of celibacy, in 1989. *Man*, she whispered. *Twenty-five years.* Next was a list of his best-selling books on spirituality and the names of his famous devotees (stars of the most valuable variety: movie, rock, sports), his dietary preferences (vegan), and his "deep interest" in astrology (Bingo was an Aquarius). He called his devotees his "roses," citing the flower as the one his grandmother loved most. Kelly read and re-read the page. She opened a new window in her browser and ordered his latest title, *Roaring Heart of Peace*, from Amazon. The book's summary enticed her with its promise: "We are energy. Physical, emotional and intellectual energy. The energy originates from in an internal territory I can help you access and explore. The exploration will lead to the wholesale demolition of the draining images and beliefs that dominate you. This work is hard and it hurts. You will be demolished."

Kelly closed the book and straightened the bowls and brushes and glass jars on the counter in her treatment room.

She dimmed the overhead and light and smoothed the table's crisp sheets. Kelly was an esthetician. She worked in a day spa in a neighborhood near Rice University whose clientele was a mixture of forty-something blondes who played serious tennis, and sorority girls with gold cards. Kelly was a fixer. She tended to emergency acne eruptions and soothed secret eyelift scars. Her specialty was working with brides, and she took a stern approach in getting them ready for their big day.

"Your skin is rough. All of this," she ran an index fingertip around the orbital bone of a new client, scheduled to marry in four months, "should not look this way. If you're squinting, you must get glasses and wear them." She drummed her fingers down the woman's tanned cheekbone. "These spots will take a long while to fade. I can get you peeled and balanced and looking fresher for the wedding, but you will need to protect your skin and do exactly what I tell you to do." Kelly moved the magnifying light away and removed a pair of cotton pads from the woman's eyes. She noticed that the pads were soggy and smeared with mascara. "It's okay. We all cry when we make a mess of our skin. Let me wax your brows, it'll make you feel better."

Kelly's personality was not beloved by her clients, but they bought everything she recommended and booked appointments months in advance because of her remarkable talent for working on faces. One of the strategies she regularly employed was to under-promise the result she could help a client achieve, and then pretend to modestly accept compliments and generous cash tips and the occasional elaborate flower arrangement from a relieved and overjoyed bride. She regularly gained new clients who had heard that she had "worked miracles" for a friend, and could she do the same for them? In six weeks? Her boss stayed out of her way because Kelly was a rainmaker, bringing in the highest commission and selling the most skincare products each month.

Her work had satisfied her for a decade, but she had begun to feel that there was little left to achieve. She was making enough money to live on and have some fun, and even though she thought that most of her clients were spoiled and entitled, she liked the feeling of purpose that came from knowing that she was helping them. Kelly hated ambiguity. She knew that her job had felt right for so long because it was measured out in ninety-minute increments, and each one of those increments had a measurable goal. Learning about Bingo on Oprah had ignited a certainty that she was made for work that was more meaningful, work that would reach more people.

Kelly found a picture of Bingo in waders, standing waist-deep in a marsh on his property in Mandeville. Under the sturdy suspenders, Bingo wore a dingy white thermal stained yellow at the armpits. His right hand rested on a cypress stump in the murky green-black water, and Kelly noticed that the fingers were stained black with what looked like motor oil. His left fingertips trailed the marshy surface. *Damn,* she whispered. The photo had been taken for a feature that appeared in *Yoga Journal* entitled, "Commanding Your Wishes." The article described the technique for manifesting that Bingo had developed, which he described as, "the sole purpose of my present incarnation." To Kelly, the instructions were simple. She was to hold an image in her mind of a thing or situation that she desired. "Make sure that the image represents something you truly want," Bingo had instructed in the article. "This meditation is powerful." When the object was firmly in sight, the meditator would visualize Bingo entering the scene in possession of the object. The third step was to visualize accepting the object from Bingo. "Open your eyes, then," Bingo instructed in the article, "and say aloud, forcefully, 'it is commanded.'"

Kelly wanted Bingo. When it came to relationships, she realized that she was not an easy fit. Her last boyfriend, a gentle chemical engineer she had met on an online dating site, gave up on their relationship a couple of weeks after they acknowledged a year of casual dating by meeting for coffee before work on a Monday.

"When are you going to let me spend the whole night with you? I don't even know your middle name."

"I have tight boundaries. It's Catherine. With a C."

"You're really harsh sometimes. I'm always saying the wrong thing."

"What can I say? I'm direct." She hadn't meant to chase him off. She liked being with him in almost every way. He was smart and talkative and great in bed. Kelly had had many conversations like this in her twenties and thirties with the men and women she dated. She was turning forty now, and was ready to change.

Kelly wanted a permanent connection with someone who was strong and masculine, who could bear her silences and not take her moodiness personally. Bingo would understand that she needed to feel things intensely. She would manifest a permanent connection with Bingo.

Kelly tried out the meditation with something small, to practice. She began on a Wednesday, deciding that she wanted to make two hundred and fifty dollars in tips before the end of work on Saturday, about fifty bucks above her average, she supposed. She checked her tip report when she arrived at work that day. Fifty-five dollars. Kelly went to work early for the next three mornings, and she sat on the rolling stool in her treatment room and closed her eyes in meditation for five minutes before her first client. She focused on an image of Bingo crouched in front of a campfire in full blaze, the flames reflected in the lenses of a pair of glasses balanced on the bridge of his nose. Kelly visualized herself standing just beyond the scene, and as she walked into it, Bingo noticed her and stood. Wordlessly, he walked up to her and put both of his big, rough-looking hands into the front pockets of his jeans and drew out of each of them a folded stack of bills, fastened tightly with rubber bands. Kelly held out her own hands and accepted the money. She opened her eyes.

Kelly did nothing else to make more money that week, only the meditation, which she did three times each day, the number of times Bingo had suggested in the article. She indulged herself in the occasional daydream about kissing Bingo as she massaged vitamin C serum into a client's jawline or made infinity symbols around their eyes with cream cleanser, but she changed nothing about her approach to customer service or her treatment technique. On Saturday at five o'clock, she asked Maya, the spa's receptionist, for the week's closing tip report.

"Oh, good for you," Maya turned to Kelly and whispered. "You're on top this week."

"Yeah? Over two hundred?"

"Three seventy-five." Maya clicked back to the schedule and counted Kelly's appointments. "What's your average?"

"Eighteen or twenty clients."

"Yep, eighteen. Good for you."

"It is, isn't it?"

Kelly kept up the manifesting meditation and saved her tips and product commission for three months and used all of her vacation days to go to the Roaring Heart retreat that Bingo held each year in Sedona, Arizona. The three-day intensive promised to "provide an opportunity to develop your innate potential to manifest. And to serve."

Kelly knew, more and more each day, that the experience she most desired was to follow Bingo and be near him always. She had a crush on Bingo, and at the same time, she wanted to be just like him. Reading every one of his books, listening to the audio tapes she bought for twenty-eight dollars each on his websites, and playing and re-playing videos of his lectures she found on YouTube had given Kelly a sense of focused ease she could not remember ever feeling, and she knew at last what she was meant to do. Bingo would say that Kelly had found "a desire worthy of whole-hearted pursuit." She understood that she was beginning to think like Bingo.

"When I call all of you my roses," he had explained during a recorded lecture at the Omega Institute in 1999, "I do not intend to minimize the human condition. These shells," he gestured up and down the length of his body, "are magnificent. At least, they can be." At this, he and the audience laughed lightly. "When I say that you are a rose, I mean that you are a friend. A friend of the guarded heart." Kelly didn't have many friends, and she wanted roses of her own, people who listened the way she could see people listening in the audience of the Oprah show that day, and in the audiences on the YouTube videos. "The feeling of deprivation is uncomfortable. You want a different job, a different car. You want to look nice in lovely clothes, you want to eat expensive healthy foods. I know. In some cases, we work hard and we get these things, and then we are hungry again. Other times, we work hard, and we get nothing in return, or we settle for less. Still hungry. We rename the hunger, calling it ambition or determination. When we've experienced enough of these hunger pains, we turn inside, if we're lucky. Begin by seeing with your eyes closed," he drew his hand down in front of his eyes like a curtain, "feeling the emptiness, the hunger for the things you want to see and feel." Bingo rubbed his thumb across the pads of his bunched fingers, as if he were sorting through a handful of hundred dollar bills.

The workshop would be held at the Hilton hotel in Sedona. Participants were told to register under Bingo's name, and that they would be assigned a place to stay when they arrived. *A place to stay*, Kelly thought, staring at the Roaring Heart website's workshop registration page. She had already paid the fifteen hundred dollar tuition. She minimized the page and stared into an image she had uploaded and enlarged of Bingo in meditation, posed at the entrance to an intricate outdoor labyrinth at dusk. Kelly liked the way Bingo dressed, in canvas pants or jeans with a regular-looking plaid shirt or t-shirt. She liked that he wasn't into the loose, flow-y linens that she associated with men like Wayne Dyer and Deepak Chopra. She thought they looked like yoga teachers.

Kelly had to write a letter describing exactly why she wanted to attend the workshop and send it by mail to a post office box with a New Orleans address. This detail thrilled her. Mandeville was just forty-five minutes from New Orleans, across Lake Pontchartrain. This meant that Bingo would probably be reading her letter himself. She knew that writing about the things that she really wanted might scare Bingo away, so she composed a bland, succinct letter about her reasons for attending the workshop, disguising the truth of her intentions. She signed off,

Yours in service,
Kelly C. Ames

A week before she was to leave for Sedona, Kelly got a call from Bingo's assistant, Stacey.

"We're all looking forward to seeing you this weekend. Bingo was impressed by your letter."

Kelly was flustered. She hadn't put her phone number in the letter. The workshop's registration form? "Oh good. That's good. I'm excited about being there, too."

"It will be hard work. The guarded place is where we face our hunger."

"Right. The desire. To get to the place of protection."

"And service."

"Yes, of course. Service."

"Bingo has asked that you accept his gift of a name for the retreat."

"A name?"

"Yes. Will you please go by the name Gulnar this weekend?"

"Sure. How do you spell that?"

Stacey spelled the name. "Gulnar means rose."

For the rest of the week, Kelly spent every spare moment in meditation to manifest a connection with Bingo. In her visions, he no longer pulled money from his pockets as he approached her in the firelight. He held out his empty hands and she reached for them. Bingo pulled her in and took Kelly's face in his hands saying, "Connect your roaring heart to mine now."

"It is commanded," she answered.

She spent the evenings preparing for the weekend, ironing and carefully folding clothes into her suitcase and re-reading the parts of each of Bingo's books that had meant the most to her. She would be ready when Bingo asked about spirituality. There was one thing that bothered her. She had typed "woman's name Gulnar" into Google as soon as she had hung up with Stacey. Translated, it meant "pomegranate flower." She typed and retyped the word, but the only spelling that connected to a name was the one she was sure she had heard Stacey spell for her. *I'll ask him about it,* she thought. Stacey had probably misunderstood. It occurred to her that this could be the way she would become close to Bingo, to really learn from him as they fell in love. She would replace Stacey. *He'll realize she's not that sharp. I can do better than that.*

Stacey was pretty sharp, though. Kelly learned this as she announced her name at the hotel's front desk on Friday evening. She had rented a car at the airport in Phoenix and gotten turned around more than once on the three-hour drive to Sedona. By the time she arrived it was dark, and the copper and ochre canyon walls she was expecting were just black, angular shadows thrown against the night sky's deep purple. The hotel was situated off the town's main highway, and the neon signs for rock shops and restaurants she passed on her way made everything look cheap and ordinary. Kelly was tired and thirsty when she finally pulled into the hotel's parking lot. Stacey had positioned herself on a white leather couch near a revolving door at the entrance and as the receptionist clicked away on the computer in front of her, Stacey stepped over to Kelly and picked up her bag.

"Gulnar. Come with me." Stacey said her name with what sounded like genuine warmth, and she embraced Kelly before guiding her into a ballroom off the hotel's lobby.

56

The room's chandeliers were dimmed and a small stage had been erected at the back of the space, covered in layers of silken Oriental rugs. In the center, a bank of fat, lighted candles circled a squat mahogany bench. Sticks of incense fumed on a ceramic dish, and as she moved closer, Kelly felt Stacey's hand on her back, steering her away.

"Go ahead and take one of those," Stacey pointed to a pile of soft-looking shapes in a corner of the ballroom.

"Wait, what? Can I just go up to my room and put my things down first?"

"This is your room. You and the other roses will be staying here this weekend. Go on." Stacey nudged Kelly in the direction of the corner, and as she got closer, Kelly realized that what she was seeing was a pile of black sleeping bags. She picked up one at the edge of the pile and noticed that it was rolled around a flat pillow in a stiff, papery case.

"Where should I put this?" Kelly cast her glance around the ballroom. Her eyes had adjusted to the lowered light, and she could see that a few of the sleeping bags had already been rolled out, with the pillow and the owner's belongings stacked on top or off to the side.

"Anywhere is fine. You'll all be good friends soon enough."

"I want to see Bingo now."

Stacey tilted her head and gave Kelly a tight smile. "I'll tell him you've arrived." Stacey left the ballroom and Kelly sat down on her sleeping bag, still rolled into a soft barrel shape. For the first time, she began to have doubts about Bingo, and she began to doubt herself and her decision to make the trip to Sedona in the first place. *As soon as he's here, everything will be fine,* she thought. *We'll talk and it will all work out.* She closed her eyes and began to meditate. She could smell the campfire and hear the crackle of dried leaves and pine straw under her feet. *The smell of a campfire? The crackle of dried leaves? Grow up!* she thought, and then imagined the negative thought flying away on black wings, as Bingo had suggested in his book, *Protected Territory: Meditations for Guarding the Sacred Mind.* The aroma of a campfire was transformed into the sharp smell of lavender oil and cigarette smoke mixed with sweat, and she heard the whispery sound of bare feet on carpet.

"My Gulnar." When she opened her eyes Bingo was standing there, and Kelly struggled onto her feet, the sleeping bag sliding away.

"It's you." She reached for Bingo's hands, and he allowed her to clasp them for a second before letting them fall back to his sides.

"I have been asking for you for months now. And here you are." Bingo smiled, and Kelly could see that his front teeth were stained with nicotine. Bingo put his arm around Kelly and led her to the edge of the stage. "I want to talk to you in the guarded place," he glanced at the bench beyond the candles. "Will you join me there?"

"I will." Kelly felt weak with excitement. *This is really going to happen.*

Bingo sat on the bench and pulled Kelly onto his lap, holding her close and kissing her cheek. "Do you know why I call you Gulnar?"

"Because you want me to be one of your roses? It means rose?" she asked, not wanting to disturb the moment of absolute contentment, the thrill of being close to Bingo at last.

"My darling, you know much better that that. What does Gulnar mean?" He brushed Kelly's bangs off her forehead, trailing his sandpaper fingertips down her cheek.

"Pomegranate flower."

"Yes. And have you ever seen a pomegranate? It's center?"

"I think so."

"Alright. Well, you know a pomegranate has a sturdy skin, a rind that guards what is inside. And what is inside a pomegranate, Gulnar?"

"Hundreds of tiny little seeds. Juicy seeds."

Bingo laughed. "Yes, tiny, juicy seeds. That is what you are to me. One of these seeds."

"What do you mean?"

"I mean that I have manifested your presence here, in this guarded space, to learn to serve. Isn't that what you wrote to me?"

"Yes."

"Yes. So now you know how you came to be here with me. You thought that you manifested this moment, didn't you?" Bingo nodded and Kelly began to nod also. "You are intelligent, dear Gulnar. You see me helping people. Important people." He nodded again and Kelly nodded along. "I can't do all of that alone, you know. If one of these important people comes to me and asks for something, there's only so much I can do. I need my roses to help me. I need you, and people like you, who want to come and be with me always."

"What about the things that I want to manifest? I came to learn how to manifest more of the things that I want, too."

"You came here for this moment. I am connected to you, as you wished. What you are beginning to feel is the desire that comes with the thought of going hungry. This is the hunger."

Kelly tried to rock herself up and off of Bingo's lap, but he was holding her tight in his arms, exactly the way she'd dreamed he would. "What if I say no? I have to go home on Monday. I have a job."

"I will care for you."

"What if I leave tonight? I could just leave here."

"My Gulnar. Remember my roses who died in desire, just a few miles from here. You are contacting the desire now. Beyond the desire is protection and service. Will you manifest life beyond? Or will you -"

"Die in desire?"

"Will you?"

Sheena

A week before I moved from south Louisiana to Fayetteville, Arkansas to take a job I really wanted, I spent a long weekend in New Orleans with a woman I was seeing at the time. Her name was Susan and she was beautiful and we couldn't stand one another. Our relationship had been ending for about six months by then, and we made the two-hour drive to the city that Friday afternoon in silence.

We had spring rolls and greasy noodles for dinner at a Vietnamese restaurant with one of my old friends that night, a woman by the name of Tammy who was always trying to put the make on my girl. Tammy brought a couple of other women with her, cool blonde femmes in sundresses and heels who spent the evening acting like her groupies. Tammy used to own a gay bar in the French Quarter. She owns a crummy gift shop in the French Quarter now, close to Canal Street, where it always smells like garbage and daiquiri vomit.

I wanted to go to an art gallery on Julia Street after dinner and buy a silver and turquoise bracelet I had seen there the last time Susan and I were in town. I had called the owner that afternoon before we left and asked her to put it behind the counter for me. She promised to hold it until ten o'clock that night when the gallery closed. Tammy mentioned that she and the blondes were driving out to the suburbs to watch a drag show and she invited Susan and me.

"That sounds boring. I want my bracelet," I whispered into my girlfriend's ear. She said that we could do whatever I wanted since it was my last time in the city until who knows when. December, at least. This happened in July of 2012.

Tammy and her friends tried to convince us to go with them to the bar for an hour or so. It was early yet, and they mentioned that it wasn't going to just be drag queens; Sheena was going to be there, too. I asked them what they meant by that, who was Sheena? They said I would have to see for myself. "Alright," I said. "One hour." Tammy paid for everyone's dinner.

I want to explain this so that you can see it. The bar was a crumbling cinder block wreck on a service road off I-10, just a few minutes outside New Orleans proper. It had an industrial-sounding name that I have forgotten, and it has probably changed hands and scenes and names a few times since. We had to park down the street at an AutoZone because the little bitty parking lot was overflowing with white Camaros and black Tahoes and a VW bug or two with the fake flowers and fuzzy dice. The works.

Of course the inside was dim and smelled like smoke. The walls were painted flat black and there was a long bar outlined with neon tubing. A couple of handsome butches behind the bar were twisting the tops off bottles of light beer and pouring glasses of White Zinfandel. There were Jell-O shots and a frozen margarita machine and everything. The pool tables were busy and a song about how everybody's free to feel good covered the sound of cruising until it all got quiet because Sheena was being introduced by a short, hunky chick in overalls and a snapback.

Susan wanted bottled water, so I found the end of a line while she looked for Tammy and the groupies. I watched as Tammy pulled her into a side hug and patted the single chair she'd saved at the edge of the stage, and then I heard a husky voice come on over the speakers. She was working the crowd's front rows, saying, "Hey darling, you looking beautiful," and, "Mmmm, look at *you*." Sheena. I tried to get a glimpse over the shoulders of the women crowded in front of me, but all I could see was wig. The top of a Cher wig, circa "Moonstruck."

I'm leaving out something important here. In the car on the way over, Susan admitted that she knew exactly who Sheena was because a friend of hers had had an affair with Sheena back in the '80's. She mentioned that this friend had described a particular seduction technique of Sheena's that she had never forgotten, a drawn-out striptease that culminated in Sheena popping off her extra-long plastic press-on nails slowly, one at a time.

"When she got to the second pinkie nail, it was on."

"Which friend?" I asked. I think it was the combination of excitement and revulsion in my voice and on my face that caused her to demure.

"It's no one you know," she answered.

The line started moving, but it was snaking out toward the stage, so I tapped the girl in front of me on the shoulder to see if I was in the right place. She pointed across the room at the bar I thought I was heading for, now empty but for the beer cap twisters, who faced the stage with their mouths slightly open in appreciation. "What's this line, then?" I asked. "The bathroom?" The place was thick with women. My eye-line was blocked by a sea of tapered hairlines and popped collars.

"This is the line for Sheena." She held up a five with both hands and twirled it a little, like it was a bow tie she was straightening. She, and all of these other women, were already in line to tip Sheena. I heard the opening bars of "How Will I Know?" by Whitney Houston and decided that Susan could get her own water. Tammy could get Susan's water. I wasn't giving up my place in that line.

None of what I eventually witnessed squared up in my mind as drag. This woman, Sheena, was performing as herself. I finally got a clear view of her as the line fell away, revealing a stout, fifty-ish woman in heavy pancake makeup, a drape-y black kimono-style dress with silver spangles, and six-inch black patent-leather heels. She was lip-synching with every muscle in her face and neck to make up for the fact that she was mostly stationary. She had to stand still because every couple of seconds someone from the line shoved money in her hand, and then waited to get some kind of blessing. These responses seemed to be based on the enthusiasm of the tipper. Shy girls got a wink. Those who lingered got kisses on the cheek, a pat on the butt, or intense extended eye contact.

Sheena took a break and the other acts booked that night took their turns onstage, a queen in a sequined pageant dress who did a couple of minutes of standup comedy, and a drag king dressed in ripped white jeans and a tank top that showed off her arms. A bunch people sitting stage-side got up for fresh drinks or the bathroom during these acts and the line I was standing in dissolved a little, so I took the opportunity to move closer to the stage.

The drag king had worked hard at her act, precisely executing choreographed moves while covering One Direction, then Luther Vandross, and finally, "As" by Stevie Wonder. When Sheena returned, I noticed that she didn't so much dance as sort of shift her weight from side to side. She occasionally departed from the line of fans to drop wads of bills in an overturned black top hat at the corner of the stage, and she stalked through the audience, stopping to steal a sip of someone's drink and swat a hank of synthetic hair from her eye using one extra-long, French-tipped, plastic press-on nail, silently belting out hit after hit. The songs didn't exactly fit together, but no one seemed to mind that she followed up "Delta Dawn" with "No Diggity."

Sheena had changed outfits while the others performed, trading in Cher for a champagne-colored bob and a burgundy minidress with shoulder pads for "Edge of Seventeen" and "Simply the Best," the song that was playing when my turn to tip her finally came. My arms were covered in goosebumps. Standing in front of a woman with the nerve to make a living performing in drag as herself made me feel like I had some pretty high-class problems. I was so flustered that all I could think to say was, "Damn, girl, look at you. *You* are something *else.*" I handed over the only cash I had, a ten-dollar bill, and she raised an eyebrow and hooked her index finger's nail under my chin, pulling my face close to hers. The only thing separating us in that moment was her useless microphone, and she smelled like cigarettes and the face powder that had caked into the lines around her eyes and mouth. I thought that Sheena was going to kiss me and I wanted to kiss her back, right there in front of Susan and Tammy and the groupies. Instead, she ran her hand down my arm to my waist, gave my hip a couple of vigorous smacks, and sent me on my way.

When I finally made it over to where Susan was sitting, she was pissed off and ready to leave. "Your bracelet? Remember?"

It was after nine by then, and I knew we'd never make it back uptown before the gallery closed at ten. "Let's stay a minute. Don't you want to say hello to Sheena?"

"No. I'm tired. And I'm quite sure she doesn't remember me." Something in the way she emphasized "me" let me know that she was the one who had slept with Sheena, not some friend of hers. She had been the recipient of the press-on nail seduction, and I was jealous.

Porcelain Doves

Carrie likes to dress like Julie. It costs ninety-five dollars to look at a picture of Julie for an hour. For the better part of sixty minutes once a week, Carrie is able to cut her eyes in the direction of the bookshelf where the picture sits, it's frame spanning the spines of *You Can Heal Your Life* by Louise Hay and a hardback copy of Pema Chodron's *No Time to Lose*.

Julie is Theresa Thurston's daughter. Theresa is a therapist Carrie has been seeing for anxiety; she was in two car accidents in a week's time and then she had a nervous breakdown. She was crying every day at work in the bathroom and sometimes at her desk. She was going broke because her boss kept sending her home.

Carrie was too afraid to drive after the accidents. She asked her gynecologist for some head medicine and he gave her one that made her more anxious, and then he gave her another one that made her hungry every minute of the day and night. She would wake up at three o'clock in the morning and walk straight to her kitchen and stand in front of the pantry shoving handfuls of granola or Chips Ahoy! or saltines into her mouth. She had to ask her mother for some cash to get new black pants for work because she had gone up two sizes all at once. Instead, her mother came to Carrie's apartment and threw away all of the crunchy carbs in the pantry and the hungry-making pills and told Carrie that she wasn't going to drive her around anymore and that she needed to get a grip.

"Mom, I have to get to work."

"Drive yourself there in the car downstairs, Carrie." She picked up Carrie's key ring. "One of these will start the engine. I am positive that you haven't forgotten how to do it."

"That's ugly."

Carrie's mother took her to Target and bought her some new pants and a belt. She told Carrie that she would pay for her to go to therapy until she felt better about driving.

"Call Theresa. She helped Teddie so much, remember?" Teddie was Carrie's older sister. She'd had an abortion in high school, which had resulted in a lot of guilt and dead baby nightmares. Theresa had helped her get over that.

Carrie thought that Theresa was pretty, which made her trust Theresa automatically. She noticed that Theresa was wearing clothing that she had seen in the Sundance catalog that showed up in her mailbox every few months, addressed to the apartment's previous occupant. Carrie left the catalog in the bathroom, and by the time she threw it away when the new one arrived, she had memorized the colors and prices of the pieces of rustic-looking clothing and jewelry she liked the best. Carrie knew that Theresa was wearing the *Serengeti Wrap Skirt* in *Olive* with her distressed-looking cowboy boots embroidered with blue and red flowers. *Bonnie,* Carrie thought when she saw the boots. *Supple cocoa and copper leather. Genuine brass accents. Five-hundred twenty dollars. Runs true to size.*

"Nice boots."

"Thank you, Carrie. Why don't we start with the car accidents? Tell me about those." Theresa glanced over the thick, stapled packet of paperwork Carrie had filled out in the waiting room.

"Right now? Just get into it?"

"Sure."

"The first one wasn't that bad. I got rear-ended. A lady slammed me during rush hour."

Theresa tapped the end of her pen on a legal pad laid across her lap. "Say more about that."

"She asked me not to call the police, but my bumper was all jammed up. My gut was like, call the cops."

"Your intuition?"

"I guess. Anyway, the policeman found out that she didn't have any insurance, and he told her I was going to sue her to fix my car."

"Did you?"

"No. My insurance company did. So yes, I did. The cop was so hard on her about it, though. She was just this sad sort of lady. I mean, she just looked like a lonely lady who smokes and buys lottery tickets. She looked divorced."

Theresa laughed. "You've made up a story about this woman. Why is that?"

"She had these faded tattoos. One was a unicorn, and the other was a pot of gold on a cloud with a lopsided rainbow shooting out of it. I think it wasn't always lopsided, though? Like, maybe she had gained weight? I'm not sure if that answers the question you asked."

"Why did those details stand out to you? Her tattoos?"

"They were around her ankles. I couldn't look at her face when she started crying."

Carrie looked away from Theresa then and saw the picture for the first time. An 8x10 black and white, the image described a woman in a black t-shirt with long sleeves seated on the floor of a bare space. Her knees were drawn up to her chest, and her slender arms wrapped around them. She noticed that the girl wore a stack of skinny silver-y bangles on her right wrist, and that her flared jeans ended in finely boned bare feet, crossed and slightly tensed. The nails were square and they looked shiny, buffed. Carrie thought that those feet looked as soft and clean as a glass of milk.

She imagined that the girl in the picture was the kind of person who would crave just an apple and a cup of green tea for lunch. She supposed that the girl could drive herself anywhere and feel just fine, and if a photographer surprised her and said *take your shoes off honey*, she would throw her head back and laugh as she did it because her feet looked like a matched set of porcelain doves, not a couple of busted softballs.

Theresa asked Carrie about the other accident then, and Carrie acted like the idea of talking about it would be too upsetting. "Can we start there next time? I can't right now. Next Monday."

When she got home, Carrie went straight to her closet. She pressed back hanger after hanger of dress pants and skirts until she found the two pairs of jeans she owned. One was a size eight and one was a twelve. She pulled out the twelve. She didn't usually wear jeans, just work clothes or leggings, and she had a couple of dressy dresses for dates.

The black t-shirt was easy, there was a solid stack of those, all kinds, including two that looked exactly like the one she had seen the girl in the photo at Theresa's office wearing. One of the t-shirts was faded and stretched out at the bottom seam. She had overstretched it after accidentally putting in the dryer instead of hanging it. The sound of the tight thread in the hem of a t-shirt breaking was satisfying, but the shirt was never as nice after. The other black t-shirt was smooth and still inky black. She laid it on top of the jeans.

When Carrie woke up the next morning and saw the outfit set out, she got excited. She rubbed lotion on her feet and squared off her toenails with an emery board. She was positive that all of this was going to help her have a better day. She planned to kick off her clogs while she was sitting at her desk.

At the end of their session, Theresa had asked Carrie if she wanted to start driving again, and Carrie said she did. She decided to drive herself to work that morning for a change, which would mean having to pass the intersection where one of the accidents had happened, the second one. She knew her only option was to gut it out, so she left home and hour early. *Just saddle up and ride*, she whispered, and started the car's ignition. She rewarded herself with a cigarette when she pulled into the parking lot.

Carrie worked in the office of a Methodist church, answering the phone and making schedules for the rest of the staff. She fixed coffee in the mornings and everybody liked it.

She turned the radio on before her colleagues came in, tuned to classical music on NPR. Sometimes she brought donuts or biscuits and links of boudin to share for breakfast. Carrie liked doing things that made the office feel homier, and no one could say that she wasn't good at her job when she was feeling okay.

Her best friend at work was a woman named Betsy who was in charge of religious education and had recommended Carrie for the job in the first place. Betsy and Carrie had been together for two years in their early twenties, and then broke up when they realized that they were mostly just good friends who wanted to sleep with other people. That was five years ago. Betsy had been the one driving Carrie to work most mornings, and to some of the other places she needed to go. Carrie and Betsy ate lunch together every day at work, and sometimes they still slept together. No one at the office knew the specifics of their history, but it was assumed that Betsy was gay because she had a brush cut and liked to wear button downs and khakis to work. From time to time, one of her co-workers or the ladies who volunteered at the church would ask Carrie if she was seeing anyone, if they could set her up with their brother or nephew or son. She supposed they thought she was straight because her hair brushed the tips of her shoulder blades and she wore dresses or skirts with sandals or boots to work. Carrie wore perfume everyday, Coco Mademoiselle. Betsy smelled like fabric softener.

"You look nice today," Betsy said at lunch. "How was your thing with the therapist?"

"Theresa. She listened to me. I can tell she was listening."

"That's good. I'm worried over here. I want you to be okay." Betsy said all of this casually, as if she was telling Carrie how she spent her weekend, with her eyes on the chicken salad sandwich on the table in front of her. Betsy and Carrie were alone in the break room, where anyone could walk in to use the microwave or the Coke machine.

69

Carrie stirred her peach yogurt. "I am going to be a-okay, don't you worry."

"Are you sure?"

"I think so. I feel good today. I drove here."

Theresa wanted Carrie to start talking about the second car accident right away at her next appointment.

"It was so much worse. That lady was poisonous. She was evil."

"Did she run into you?"

"Yes."

"On purpose?"

"It was an accident, but she ran a red light and tried to blame me for the wreck." Carrie realized that if she was going to tell this upsetting story to Theresa, she could use the opportunity to act as if eye contact would be too much. She could turn her face toward the bookshelves that lined the office wall and pretend that she was interested in the titles of the books there. She could look at the photograph.

"How did she do that, Carrie?"

"She flew out of her little truck raising hell. The first thing she said was that I crossed into her lane. Then she said I turned on red without yielding first."

"And how was that personal?"

She turned her face toward Theresa again. "I'm getting to that." Carrie noticed that Theresa was wearing the same boots as last time, with *Open Road Patchwork Pants. Light Coral Pink.* She has money, Carrie thought. A lot of money. *Ninety-eight dollars.*

"Carrie, you seem upset right now. Would you like some water?"

Carrie focused on the picture. She had come to the appointment straight from work and she was hungry. She wanted something salty, like a biscuit from Popeye's. A three-piece spicy box with mashed potatoes and an extra biscuit. She imagined that the girl in the picture never ate fast food. Maybe she ate a Popeye's drumstick on Mardi Gras day. She probably thought chicken on the bone was disgusting. "No, thank you."

Theresa took a tube of hand lotion from the table next to the chair where she was sitting and squeezed a bit into her hand. "Carrie, are you sure that the woman who hit you wasn't just feeling shaken up herself? Would that explain her behavior?" The size of a pea, Carrie thought. Theresa is the person who actually uses a pea-sized amount of lotion.

"I don't know how she felt. She was shouting and pointing at me and her face was all red when I turned my back to call the police. She stopped yelling after that."

"But I heard you say that she was poisonous and evil. What did she do that indicated that those things were true?"

"I just told you."

Theresa opened her mouth and then closed it again with a sigh. It was a look that Carrie recognized. Her sister Teddie made the same face when she was about to say something true in a sharp tone of voice and then decided to say something true very slowly instead. "Carrie, I've noticed that you tend to create stories around stressful events, adding in details that may or may not be grounded in reality. Remember when you told me that the other woman who hit your car looked divorced?"

"She was giving me that vibe, big time. If you had seen her, you would get it."

"That's an example of the storytelling I am talking about. I would like to help you understand why you feel the need to do this, and then we can work on some coping skills to replace that behavior."

"I'm not lying. I feel like you're saying that I'm lying and I'm not. All of this happened." Carrie gathered her cardigan and started digging in her purse for her car keys. "I'm already getting better, anyway. I drove here." She located her keys and held them up for Theresa to see.

"That's great news. I'd still like to talk to you about some strategies you can use to help you deal with your anxiety around driving and other stressful situations. Times when you are having trouble telling the difference between what you're thinking or feeling and the truth of what really happened. Or, in some cases, what did not happen."

Carrie bit her bottom lip to keep from snapping at Theresa and then snapped at her anyway. "Look, forget it."

"You're frustrated."

"What do you think?"

At the end of the session, Theresa gave Carrie some suggestions for helping with her anxiety. "Whenever you encounter a challenge, or when a situation feels stressful, I would like for you to pause and look at your hands. Remind yourself that your hands are in the present moment, even though your imagination may want to escape to the future or the past. Try to remember to stay where your hands are."

"That sounds like woo-woo nonsense, Theresa. That sounds like AA. I am the challenge, my brain is what is challenging me."

"It's a place to start. Try."

Even though Theresa's pushing made her feel frustrated, Carrie had been looking forward to their session, and she had thought about Theresa sometimes during the week and wondered what her life was like. She assumed that the girl in the photo was Theresa's daughter; they had the same long limbs and oval-shaped face. Carrie wondered what it would be like to have Theresa as a mother. She'd probably given the girl the silver bracelets she was wearing in the photo as a birthday gift. Theresa probably had a set for herself that the girl had admired, so she wanted her daughter to have some of her own. Carrie imagined that the girl put the bracelets on every day out of habit, because she was close to her mother and liked feeling connected to her that way. She probably admired her mother's taste.

The result of Carrie's examination of her "challenges" was an urge to quit her job immediately. In terms of stress, the drive to work was kicking her ass the most.

"I'm thinking about moving on," Carrie whispered to Betsy the next morning at the coffee pot.

"Let's talk at lunch."

The phone was quiet that morning, so Carrie scanned the openings for admin jobs on Craigslist and wrote down the ones she was most qualified for. Three of them were within a mile of her apartment, and she could walk or ride her bike there if she was having a bad day. She wondered if she could wear jeans and black t-shirts in the offices that needed receptionists. She crossed a few off the list, doctor's offices and a day spa. She would have to wear a uniform to work at those places. And shoes. Her black Converse lay untied on the floor under her desk. She wanted more shirts, and one pair of jeans was not enough. She had worn the outfit on Saturday and Sunday, and she was worried that her jeans wouldn't be dry in time for work on Tuesday. *Might as well get some new ones while I'm still getting paid,* she thought. She clicked over to the Gap's website and began adding black long-sleeved t-shirts and pairs of size-twelve bootcut jeans into her cart until it was time to meet Betsy for lunch.

"You need to know where you're going before you take off, Carrie. Have you found something else?"

"No, but I'm good at getting jobs."

"Why do you want to start over? You've gotten really good at holding this show together."

Carrie laughed. "Right. I've memorized everyone's coffee order and I *cher-cher* you all. I put up with a lot of shit."

"Can you please just wait until vacation Bible school is over? I'm really gonna need you."

"Maybe."

"Why don't you let me cook dinner for you tonight? I've got some shrimp to boil."

"Maybe."

"How's the driving going? Are you checking in with your hands?" Theresa asked at the beginning of Carrie's third session.

73

"I guess."

"You're still driving, right?"

"Yes. To work and my mom's and Betsy's. The grocery store. Here. I got myself here, too."

"Betsy is?"

"A friend. We work together. We dated a little bit, but we're mostly friends."

"Mostly?"

"People need people, Theresa."

Carrie was tired of wondering who the girl in the picture was. At the end of the hour, as Theresa scheduled her next appointment, Carrie noticed a new framed picture of the same young woman on Theresa's desk.

"She's a pretty girl."

"My daughter, Julie. That was taken last New Year's."

In the picture on Theresa's desk, Julie wore a short black cocktail dress. In one hand she held a half-full flute of champagne, and with the other she aimed a lighted Roman candle, mid-explosion, at the night sky. She had knotted her platinum hair into a bun at her crown like a ballerina and her teeth were bright as chalk against lips painted a deep matte red. Theresa swiveled her chair to face Carrie and the new picture disappeared.

"See you next Monday."

That night, Carrie twisted her hair into a bun and slicked on the closest thing she had to red lipstick, a fingerful of cream blush she had gotten in a free gift bag from the Lancome counter at Macy's. She sat down at her computer and typed *black cocktail dresses* into the search bar and ordered five of the least expensive ones that looked like the dress Julie was wearing in the New Year's Eve photo. She felt calm enough then to do the new exercise Theresa had given her, adding three places to the list she had made the week before, three new places she could drive to. Theresa had suggested that Carrie sit in her car for a moment before she put the key in the ignition and look at her hands.

74

"Focus on the destination. When you feel your mind beginning to shift into a narrative of what could happen, remind yourself that the story hasn't happened. The story is not real, Carrie."

"Okay. I know."

"When you get to your destination, reflect on the real story of the journey. Think about what really happened."

"I'll do it. I can try."

The dresses came in the mail one by one for the next ten days, and Carrie kept the ones that made her look smaller. She went to the drugstore and bought two tubes of matte red lipstick. One was too orange, and she decided she would save it to wear in the summer. There would be new black dresses in her closet by then. The other lipstick was better, more scarlet than vermillion. She hung the dresses in her closet beside the new pairs of jeans.

Quitting the office was easy, mostly because of the technique Theresa had taught her. Whenever she started feeling overwhelmed, she would look at her hands and check in with the present. This was how she realized that when she was at work, the present was dull and frustrating. The present she experienced at work was causing her to feel stressed and make up stories. She had to quit.

She snuck the personal stuff from her desk home a little at a time over a couple of days, and then went in thirty minutes early on Friday with a box of hot donuts. She grabbed a Sharpie from the jar of pens on her desk and printed her resignation on the top of the box. *Bye, guys. Sorry.*

Of course, there were phone calls. Her boss, Tommy, left a tense-sounding voice mail: *Carrie, if you need some time off to rest, you can have as much as you need...we all care about you.* This caring infuriated her somehow. She was already feeling better. *You can come and talk to me, Carrie. Please, just don't quit like this.* Betsy called. *I'm in the weeds because of you right now, can you get back to me with your log in, please? Like, right now.* Carrie texted Betsy her passwords and then turned her phone off.

75

The next thing she did was print a handful of flyers advertising herself as a housekeeper, a job she had had in college. She was good at cleaning, baseboards and everything, and surveying a newly organized space had always made her feel serene. This work made the most sense because could wear the same thing every day, like a uniform. Wearing Julie's clothes would make her look professional. *You're supposed to take your shoes off before you clean house anyway,* she thought.

She took the flyers to the health food store and tacked some up, and she took a few over to the public library to put on the bulletin board there. While she was there, she searched the shelves for her favorite book on cleaning and organizing. She'd borrowed it a half dozen times, but her conscience wouldn't let her buy it because it cost fifty bucks.

"It's called *Homekeeping,*" she said to the librarian at the reference desk. "Martha Stewart. I only saw the bridal books on the shelf, but the catalog says you have it." The woman frowned at her computer screen, and then tabbed and tabbed and tabbed over. "It says it's in. Oh, wait. It's on hold for another patron."

"Can I look on the carts back there? I think I see it. It's big. One of the big ones at the bottom." Carrie pointed in the direction of four rolling carts behind the desk, loaded with books.

"Those books are on hold for other patrons."

"I'll just be a minute. I just want that Martha Stewart book and that's all."

"Ma'am, I'm sorry."

"You don't need to call me ma'am, you're older than me. Look, I'll just check it out overnight, okay? What are the chances that the person who asked for it is going to come and get it in the next," Carrie looked at her watch, "thirty minutes? You close at six, right? They'll never know. Now let me by." Carrie started to push past the woman.

The librarian had one of the male clerks escort Carrie to her car. Without *Homekeeping.*

Carrie didn't let the library incident slow her down. She had about two hundred dollars saved, and she wanted to leave that alone, so she needed to start making money cleaning houses right away, since she had blown so much of her final paycheck on new clothes. She called her mother.

"I'm trying something different. Can you call some of your friends and tell them that I'm cleaning houses now? Your granite counter-top friends. From tennis."

"When do you have time to do that?"

"My schedule at work is going to be more flexible. I can work in the mornings and clean in the afternoon." She would tell her mother about quitting when she was making money again.

"You can come over here one day a week and clean. I'll pay you ten an hour for that."

"Please tell your friends and anyone else that you know a dependable maid who won't steal their magazines or smoke in their bathroom and give them my number. Please?"

Carrie's mother paid her to clean her condo twice and then fired her for cutting into a pan of lasagna she had made for a potluck.

Being completely unemployed caused less anxiety than Carrie had imagined, and she believed that this was because the clothes were working. She was able wear the black dresses more, and she really went for it with the makeup. Wearing the dresses gave her the most relief. She fell asleep on her couch one evening in her favorite one, a knee-length wrap-around in heavy jersey. *Obsidian* was the color, according Nordstrom's website. It was so comfortable that she started putting it on before bed a few nights a week. She used box of color from the drugstore to give herself what she thought would be platinum streaks through her crown that would show up nicely when she scraped her hair into a bun. The result was brassy, but she liked the difference, and resolved to use a lighter color next time. She had plenty of time to get it right. She was feeling the way she thought a blonde would feel, and she was getting better at making a crisp, tight line with her black liquid eyeliner. Practicing that had taken an entire afternoon.

She was dragging her recycling to the curb in the comfy *Obsidian* dress early the next Monday morning when Betsy pulled into the vacant parking spot next to her car.

"You're all dressed up. Funeral?"

"Interview. Why aren't you at work?" She hadn't seen Betsy since she quit her job.

"I have a dentist appointment at nine. I took the morning off. What time's the interview?"

"It's on Thursday. I was just trying on outfits. I'm about to fix myself a waffle. Do you want one?" Betsy had a waffle with peanut butter and rescheduled her dentist appointment from Carrie's bed.

"I'm still mad at you for running out on the office, you know." Betsy pulled Carrie into the crook of her arm and slapped Carrie's bare ass with her other hand. "I could spank you."

"Who's at my desk now?"

"No one, we're juggling it. Tommy wants you to come back. Because he is crazy."

"Is that why you're here?"

"Yeah, I thought I'd seduce you and then ask you to come back to work. Get serious. I don't want you to come back." Betsy rolled onto her side so that Carrie couldn't see her face.

Carrie propped herself up on a stack of pillows and scratched Betsy's back. "Tommy misses me. Tommy misses my coffee. I'm not coming back, don't worry. I want a new life, from scratch. I want to start all the way over."

Carrie wore regular work clothes, khakis or a dress, on Mondays for her appointments with Theresa. She couldn't decide if telling Theresa about leaving her job would make things better or worse, so she decided to leave it alone. Her mother was covering the hour, and as soon as Carrie sat down on the couch, she was able to forget her worries about driving and the bills stamped SECOND NOTICE that she had torn in half and thrown away at the first of the month. Looking at the pictures in Theresa's office each week was helping her more than the therapy, she thought.

Carrie would say something like, "I've been checking the mirror less, but I'm still so jumpy," at the beginning of her sessions with Theresa. Something like that. She wanted Theresa to know that she still needed her.

"Have you practiced the visualization technique we talked about?"

"Yes. That's helping, I think." *Rose Glory dress. Elegance and whimsy make this floaty chiffon blend sheath's effortless chic a best bet for work and play. Fully lined. One hundred seventy-eight dollars.*

Theresa had given up on trying to get Carrie to stop building stories. Instead, she had asked Carrie to mentally rehearse each trip she took in her car, even if it was just a minute down the road for cigarettes. She was supposed to sit in the driver's seat with her hands on the steering wheel and close her eyes. Theresa told Carrie to leave her keys on the dashboard and envision driving with her eyes directly on the road in front of her, and to imagine arriving at her destination completely safe and contented.

Carrie had practiced the exercise a few times, and when she closed her eyes, she imagined driving straight to Theresa's office. When she opens the door, Theresa isn't there, but Julie is. Carrie sits in Theresa's chair, since Julie is sitting on the couch where Carrie usually sits. She says, *I've never really liked the name Julie.* Carrie taps the end of a pen on one of Theresa's legal pads and says, what about Carrie? Do you like the name Carrie?

To Yoke

Nothing was missing from Sheila Gardner's life. Nothing was wrong.

"I mean, there's nothing wrong," she told her mother over the phone one Sunday. "I'm just not that happy."

"You'll meet someone, honey, don't worry. It's all about timing."

"It's not even that. I'm not lonely, I have a social life. I date."

"Yes, and you have a great job and a nice little condo. You've always been my go-getter, baby." Her mother was proud of Sheila's job as a lawyer and the tasteful clothes and possessions that she bought with her big salary. She didn't understand that Sheila got dressed up every morning in a sleek suit and drove her sleek BMW downtown and then sat at a desk and did paperwork and made phone calls all day, and that her work wasn't special and exciting. Sheila didn't get to righteously yell at anyone in court like the lady lawyers on television. Sheila didn't get to go to court.

Her mother couldn't understand that the best part of Sheila's day was the ninety minutes she set aside to practice yoga at Leaping Deer Studio. She had signed up for a series of beginner classes a year before to relieve some of the tension that had accumulated in her neck and shoulders from hours of sitting in front of a computer at work, as well as a nasty bout of insomnia that had been plaguing her since she'd earned the promotion she had doggedly fought for, alienating herself from most of her colleagues in the process.

Moving through the poses, which she now knew to call asanas, in the heated studio had freed her wrenched trapezius and strained scalenes at last. She was finally sleeping soundly, and the rigor of the sequences had replaced the frantic exhaustion she felt at the end of each work day with the sensation of having been wrung out, her muscles flushed with cleaner, better blood. It was a feeling she remembered from high school, when she ran cross country.

Sheila began practicing yoga six times a week and meditating each day for twenty minutes. The practice introduced her to a community of people even more enthusiastic than she was. Sheila wanted what they had, and this was what was making her unhappy. She wanted to snap her mat open each morning and take her time moving through a practice that she had thoughtfully composed, and then spend her afternoons sipping twig tea and reading Patanjali's sutras and the philosophy of Krishnamurti. In her idea of a perfect world, she would practice again at the studio each evening and then join in the conversations she'd overheard people having in the studio that seemed so heartfelt and sincere. Conversations about Kirtan and mudras and the benefits of oil pulling. She wanted to trade her suits and heels for cozy leggings and soft sweaters made from organic fibers.

Sheila knew that all of her wanting was the cause of her unhappiness because she had read it in the little book of Buddhist tenets her favorite teacher, Marina, had given her for her thirtieth birthday. The book explained that the Buddha had said that "the cause of all suffering is desire." It was Marina who had helped Sheila envision a solution to her suffering, an answer to her new desire.

Sheila had come to class twenty minutes early to practice pressing up into a handstand from crow pose. "You're getting stronger, that's good," Marina said.

"I wish I could practice twice a day. I wish I could practice all day, actually," Sheila laughed.

"Easy, now. Excess is the enemy of contentment." Sheila admired Marina's poise, and she compared herself to Marina most of the time. They were about the same age, she figured; Marina couldn't have been older than thirty-five. She was taller than Sheila, at least 5'8, with olive skin and dark, straight hair cut in a blunt, chin-length bob. Sheila wondered when her practice would yield ropy muscles like Marina's: legs carved from marble, blocky shoulders, and forearms crisscrossed with taut veins. Even Marina's feet were muscular.

"You're right. I just love it here." The studio had become Sheila's favorite place, and she wanted to be there even more than the modern condominium she had spent three years carefully decorating in cream and camel and beige. She'd never enjoyed cooking much, and relished the new simplicity of roasting vegetables and cooking pot a of brown rice a couple of times a week for lunches and dinners since she had borrowed *The Macrobiotic Way* from the studio's bookshelf. Leaping Deer was the opposite of her space at home, warm and funky and smelling of chandan incense. At first, Sheila thought the place was kind of sloppy, especially the lobby, where piles of sandalwood malas competed with gauze-y scarves and pricey yoga mats and the thin, colorful towels the students laid on top of the mats to absorb the thick rivulets of sweat that dripped off their limbs during class. Sheila owned three of those, in various shades of pink.

"Have you thought about teaching?" Marina asked as Sheila slowly came out of handstand, carefully placing one foot, and then the other, onto her mat.

"I wish. My job."

"Choices. I get it. You would have to make some sacrifices."

"It would be so dreamy, though."

"Think it over. You can get certified in a couple of months. It's just two hundred hours of training."

"A couple of months away from work? I don't think I could."

"No vacation days over there?"

"Oh, I have so many. I never take leave." It was true. Sheila had six weeks of vacation a year, plus enough sick days to recover from any cold or flu virus a dozen times over. "I guess I could check into it."

Within a month, Sheila had arranged to take all of her vacation days to attend a teacher training at an ashram in

82

Massachusetts that specialized in Ashtanga yoga, which was closest to what Marina taught at Leaping Deer. The senior partners at her firm were understanding, and told her that she would be missed, especially since her team had taken on a new corporate project. She was also told in no uncertain terms that either she or her letter of resignation would be expected in the office within six weeks.

After she was certified, Marina helped Sheila get a gig teaching beginner classes at Leaping Deer three nights a week. This responsibility thrilled her and made her hungry for more. She returned to her job with real resentment, working only sixty-hour weeks and turning off her cell phone from Friday evening until Monday morning. Her boss noticed and moved a colleague she was supervising into her place on three of her major projects.

"I'm okay with it," she told Marina one Saturday morning after an advanced Vinyasa class. "Being here is more important to me."

"It's funny how perspectives change, isn't it?" Marina put her hand at Sheila's sacrum. "Let's try standing back bend. Let your fingertips lead you up and over. Up and over like a candy cane." Sheila's fingers reached the floor. "Good girl," Marina said, and helped her up.

Sheila had begun working at the studio's front desk before and after class on weekends, checking students in and sending email blasts about upcoming workshops and special pricing. She noticed that the wording of the ads was often sloppy and unprofessional, so she fixed that. She rearranged the merchandise in the lobby, and threw away all of the 10 and 20 percent off price tags. *These people have money to spend,* she thought. *Discounts just make you wonder.* She moved the most expensive leggings to the front table and laid out the newest headbands and hair ties in coordinating colors beside each folded stack.

Sheila found more flaws in the way the studio operated, things that weren't obvious when she was only a student. Aside from the slipshod marketing, she realized that the relationships between teachers were competitive and contentious, and their personal habits were horrifying. When she wondered out loud why there was a row of lockers in the laundry room, Caroline, the girl who kept up with the studio's towels in exchange for free classes explained that there had been an ongoing problem with theft in the studio. "These people are disgusting, okay? No boundaries. When I started, I kept finding pairs of sweaty leggings and tank tops stuffed in the bottom of the towel basket in the locker room, right? Nice, name brand shit. I wash and fold them, put them in the lost and found like I'm supposed to. A couple of days go by and someone comes in asking if their clothes have turned up, and of course they're not there anymore. Then, a week or two after that, Marina shows up in the top or the leggings. This has happened, like, three separate times. She goes in there and scoops up whatever she wants while these people who pay her to teach them how to find serenity and get their shit together are in the shower. Don't ever leave your stuff on the benches in the locker room while you shower."

"No. That can't be right," Sheila swallowed hard. "Right? No way."

"Ever seen the lost and found shelf? Ponytail holders and busted sunglasses. Come on, girl. Wake up. She shops there regularly."

"Oh, no."

"Don't let Cedar adjust you in class. He'll find any excuse to adjust your hips during half pigeon, right? He goosed me once, and I got up and left. I was pissed."

Sheila stood there with her mouth open. "He's really into working on hip openers and glutes, right? Isn't he a runner?"

"Who gives a shit? He's not practicing, the class is. It's messed up, Sheila."

Sheila knew she had to make a change when she overheard Marina in the studio's kitchen one morning, talking to Laurel, one of the senior Vinyasa teachers.

"I am so tired of listening to the same sob stories," Marina emptied a packet of instant oatmeal into a mug and turned on a flame under the kettle. "Like, I get it: you had a miscarriage. Get over it, please."

"Who's this again?" Laurel asked.

"My Tuesday, Thursday 9:30. I mean, she's got it made. She drives a Benz, she doesn't work. She cries every session."

"Poor thing," Laurel said, and rolled her eyes. "Give her to Cedar. Why are we the ones always working mornings when it's dead?"

"Those private sessions are my bread and butter, though. She gave me a five hundred dollar tip last year at Christmas. They put Cedar on evening classes because he's pretty. Have you seen his Friday night class? Cougars, wall to wall. On the prowl." Sheila couldn't believe what she was hearing, and she couldn't believe Marina would say those things where she could hear them. A boundary had dissolved between them now that Sheila was no longer just a client, but she had imagined that becoming Marina's colleague would make her admire her more. She cancelled the private session she'd scheduled with Marina that day and went home early. "I'm feeling sick to my stomach all of a sudden," she said.

One Saturday she stayed late to work on handstands and thirty minutes into her practice she heard the string of brass bells attached to the front door jingle, and then the ding of the cash register opening. "Hello," she called.

"Just me and Cedar." It was Marina. Sheila lowered her legs and eased onto her back on the mat. Through the gauze curtains that separated the studio from the lobby, she could see Cedar thumbing through a stack of bills.

"Forty-five," she heard him say.

"That's it?" Marina.

"Yeah, but happy hour lasts until seven. So what's that? Three margaritas each? Plus a tip?"

Sheila laid in Savasana for a long time after she heard the bells jingle again, and then she rolled up her mat and went to the front desk and did something she'd been resisting for two weeks. She composed a new email to every client who had ever visited Leaping Deer, announcing the opening of Fawn, Leaping Deer's sister studio. She listed the opening date three weeks out and promised a month of free classes for the first fifty people through the studio door. She closed with the studio's contact information: her cell phone number and the address of her condo.

She had always been careful with her paycheck, and her lackluster social life had left her savings in good shape. She figured that she had enough to buy all of the necessities for the studio, plus a little left for marketing and insurance. The email had given her a reason to scramble to get Fawn ready to open, and the first thing she did was order a small painted sign to hang on her front door. She liked feeling like her studio would be a secret place, hidden in plain view. She'd have to be careful and take the sign down after class each evening, or the condo association would nix her plan. The complex was zoned strictly residential.

She gave notice at the firm and asked HR to help her cash in her 401K. Two weeks later, she packed up her desk and left without fanfare. She had confided in few people in the six years she'd worked there, never joining her colleagues for drinks at the close of major projects. She understood that the isolation she had felt at work was a direct result of her lack of awareness of her real vocation, teaching yoga. Underneath this realization was a desire she was only just beginning to acknowledge: Sheila wanted to do more than teach yoga, she wanted the practice to sweep into every tight, unsatisfying corner of her life like a warm wave, dragging away her old possessions, beliefs and ideas, replacing them with a transformed existence. Sheila wanted to *be* yoga.

She advertised her BMW for sale on Craigslist and then she called her little sister and asked her if she wanted some of her furniture. "Everything in the living room and the tables in the front hall. Also, the bedroom set."

"Your new couch?" Her sister Lauren was twenty-two, and Sheila liked the way she looked up to her, asking her advice about college and clothes.

"Everything."

Surveying her mostly empty apartment that weekend as Lauren and her boyfriend loaded a U-Haul with the furniture from her living room and bedroom strengthened Sheila's resolve. She knew she had made the right decision.

"Hey, take those too, bug," she called to Lauren, sweeping her hand in the direction of the framed Jazz Fest posters and O'Keefe prints that covered the living room's back wall.

"Yeah?" Lauren asked, surprised. "Even Jerry Lee Lewis?"

"Take Jerry Lee. And those candles. I got some new ones yesterday."

"These haven't even been burned. Don't you want to save them?"

"No."

"Well, thank you. Call me when your new furniture comes. I want to see it. Where do you plan to sleep until then?" Lauren pointed in the direction of Sheila's empty bedroom.

"Oh, I might check into a hotel." When she was alone, Sheila moved the one piece of furniture she'd kept, a polished mahogany end table, to the front of the living room. On it she arranged a shrine with a pair of oranges in a wooden bowl, a tall glass with a bundle of red and yellow silk roses, a resin figurine of Ganesha, and a laminated holy card depicting St. Michael the Archangel crushing a serpent with his sandal, sword poised mid-air. She lighted a pair of small candles-peppermint and lavender-and rolled out the brand-new, double-thick mat she'd gotten at a discount when she'd bought fifty new mats wholesale. The sales rep who took her order congratulated her on opening a new studio. "It's a brave thing to do," she'd said, "and the world needs more yoga."

Sheila taught her first class at Fawn on Monday. Classes were scheduled at 7:00 a.m., noon, 4:00 p.m., and 6:00 p.m., Monday through Saturday. Sundays were reserved for extended meditation and pranayama practice. She had just finished straightening the circle of zafu cushions facing the bright turquoise and orange mandala she had painted on the east wall of what used to be her bedroom when the doorbell rang. She closed that room's door gently and hurried to let in her first students, a quartet of women in their twenties that she recognized from Leaping Deer.

"Welcome to Fawn," Sheila said, careful to keep her voice soft and even in reverence for the sacred space she had created.

"Where's the bathroom?" One of the girls pushed past her and began to wander through the space, knocking the St. Michael holy card off the altar and jiggling the candles. "My bad," she said, without breaking stride. The other ones wanted water. Sheila had expected at least twenty students, based on the number of emails and phone calls she had gotten in the weeks since she'd sent out the initial message about Fawn.

The class didn't go well. She started at 7:00 sharp, and two more people showed up late. Sheila had to stop calling out the directions for opening pranayama to let them into the studio. She left the front door cracked, making a mental note to order another small sign directing people to come in quietly if they arrived after class started. The screech of a garbage truck emptying the contents of a dumpster as she moved the class through half-moon pose startled her, and as she turned up the music and raised her voice, she hoped that her neighbors wouldn't notice or mind. She was shaky and wired by the end of the hour. After Savasana, Sheila reminded the students that they had earned a month of free classes.

"Only four classes on the schedule each day?" A student held up one of the postcard-size schedules Sheila had placed beside each of their mats.

"For now. I'm teaching them all," Sheila said. "Who would like some detox tea?"

Things smoothed out after a week of teaching. Sheila amended the schedule so that Monday morning classes began thirty minutes later, well after garbage pickup. She finally had an opportunity to practice whenever she wanted, read whenever she wanted. Her favorite part of each evening was designing and practicing a new sequence of asanas for the next day's classes.

Sheila was getting used to sleeping on the considerably smaller, thinner futon mat, and when she wasn't using her washer and dryer she draped a lavender batik shawl over them, which made the space feel homier. She thought the best part of her new life was being able to wear leggings and a tank top all day long, and she loved twisting her hair into a simple bun each morning. She'd stopped wearing makeup. She'd stopped wearing a watch, too, timing her classes by the wall clock in her kitchen, one of the few things she hadn't pushed off on Lauren.

Fawn made a little money the third week it was open. Finally, the 51st new student arrived for an evening class. It was Marina.

"We miss you at the studio," she said, taking her place at the back of the practice space. Six other students whispered to one another or lay in child's pose, waiting for class to begin.

Sheila ignored her. "Alright everyone, stand in Tadasana at the top of your mat. Engage Udiana banda and begin to initiate Ujjayi breath."

Sheila had abruptly quit working and going to classes at Leaping Deer after overhearing the exchange between Marina and Cedar. Since then, Marina had tried calling and emailing her, and she figured that Marina must have heard about Fawn from another student at Leaping Deer. She had made the possibility of a confrontation with Marina the focus of her meditation each day, imagining herself surrounded in a protective golden light as she explained her choice to move on. *The world needs more yoga*, she imagined herself saying. This helped her anxiety.

She felt distracted during the entire class that Marina attended. At one point she saw an opportunity to help Marina twist further in Marichyasana, and wondered if her teacher had intentionally held herself back from her fullest expression of the pose. *She's done that twist a million times*, Sheila thought. She placed a hand on Marina's ribs. "Breathe wide across your chest." She felt Marina's inhale beneath her palm and guided her up and back. "Twist all the way open. If its okay with your neck, you can look over your shoulder." She cued the pose as she would for any beginner. Marina lifted her chin and met Sheila's eyes and smiled.

Marina began practicing at Fawn each morning, always coming in silently and half-heartedly working even the most elementary asanas. Sheila adjusted Marina at least once every class; her conscience wouldn't allow her to let Marina injure herself. She wondered if Marina would risk a strained muscle just to run her off her feet. Or sabotage Fawn. Sheila made another mental note to double-check the specifics of the insurance policy she'd bought for the studio. And her renter's insurance, too. At the end of the practice, Marina accepted one of the paper cups of detox tea that Sheila offered to each student, rolled up her mat, and left, thanking Sheila over her shoulder.

Marina started sending students from Leaping Deer to Fawn. Lots of clients: men and women who approached Sheila before or after class to let her know that they were there on Marina's recommendation.

She thought she could fit about twenty-one students into her front room to practice, and one morning, twenty-five people showed up for class. "Okay, some of you can get set up in here," she said, opening the door to the meditation room.

"There's carpet in here," complained a woman in an orange unitard. "Gross."

Sheila felt ice cold sweat begin to form under her arms. "Maybe someone in the main practice space will switch places with you?" She asked loudly, hoping a volunteer would come forward. The rest of the class looked down at their mats or closed their eyes in faux meditation. *Shitheads,* she thought. *I bless everyone I come in contact with,* she thought next, and forgave herself for her negative projection. *Bless her. Bless them.* "Next time, come a little earlier," she suggested.

"I have children, alright? I have to get them situated before coming here. This is supposed to be my relaxation. My peace," the lady huffed.

Cleaning up after each class took almost an hour. The students left both of her bathrooms a shambles of damp hand towels and bare toilet paper rolls. There were empty teacups to collect and loaner mats to clean and re-roll and stack in the hall closet the way she liked. She walked through the room with a lighted sage stick each night to clear out the stagnant, sweaty energy and made sure the hardwood floor was clean, but not too slippery; swabbing it on her hands and knees with diluted soapsuds and vinegar worked best, she'd found. Then there were release forms to file and accounting to tend to, and research for classes. Phone calls to make and return. Her own practice was becoming rushed, and at times, rote.

Sheila's body began to rebel. A deep ache flared at the front of her left shoulder, radiating up her neck and down into her bicep each time she was in Chaturanga Dandasana, until she could no longer effectively demonstrate the pose in class. Sheila was verbally leading a series of sun salutations at a morning class when Marina got up and dragged her mat to the front of the room so that everyone could see her perfect form. Sheila squatted beside her and pointed to Marina's upper body. "Let's break this pose down. Neck is long. Gaze forward, and rotate your shoulders back and down. Now roll the elbows inward and pin them to your sides." She looked up at the ten other students in the room, recognizing the look on some of their faces. They were rapt, relieved of their more realistic concerns. The whole world was Chaturanga Dandasana.

Marina stayed after class and worked with Sheila, testing her shoulder's range of motion and assisting her in a bolstered, supine twist. "You should ice this, pronto," Marina said.

"There's a sage stick on the counter in my kitchen. Will you get it for me, please?" Sheila lighted the sage and had Marina wave the smoldering bundle around her injury. "Think it's my rotator cuff?"

"It's probably just strained." Sheila's doorbell buzzed sharply twice, followed by a hail of strong knocks on the condo's front door.

"Somebody probably forgot their sweater." It wasn't a student at the door, though. It was her neighbor, Mrs. Morgan.

"What is all of this traffic in and out of your unit?"

"Sorry, what?" Sheila was flustered by the intensity of the lady standing in front of her, the same little old lady who had brought over a plate of brownies and a grand poinsettia the week after Sheila moved into the complex.

"Is that marijuana? What is that smell? Are you smoking dope in there?"

"No, ma'am, its sage. I was burning sage to clear some energy. I hurt my shoulder."

"I'm reporting you to the association, young lady. For the past month, I have seen and heard people coming and going from your unit at all hours of the night and day. My parking space was blocked for the third time in a week this morning. Are you selling drugs?"

"Mrs. Morgan, I'm teaching yoga classes. It's nothing illegal, I swear. It's healthy!"

"This complex is residential only. I'm reporting you today."

When Sheila turned around, she saw Marina standing in the doorway of the meditation room, smirking. "What are you even doing here?" Sheila demanded. "Why are you helping me? Why have you been coming to class?" Marina began rolling up her mat. "Answer me."

"Why shouldn't I help you? You were my best student for a long time. I'm happy for you."

"You know why you shouldn't help me. All of the people you just practiced with," she flung her arm across the empty living room, "were your old clients. Which," she stabbed at the air between them with her finger, "I'm not that sorry about. I know how you feel about your regulars, I overheard you talking about them more than once."

"I'm not perfect, Sheila. Neither are you. Yoga doesn't make you into some kind of perfect person."

"I know that, Marina." Sheila was beginning to raise her voice. "It's not about perfection. It's a union, remember? To join." Sheila laced her fingers together and held them up in the space between her face and Marina's. "Joining the physical and the spiritual? Sound familiar? You're the one who taught me that. It's the definition of yoga. To yoke."

Marina nodded. "Right. I was like you in the beginning. I was on fire. I took a second and then a third job to get certifications so that I could be the best. And then one day, I was the best. Now I practice to keep my body in shape. I teach for money. That's all. That is my version of this union." Marina put air quotes around "union." She tucked her mat under her arm. "Remember what I said about excess?"

The next afternoon, Sheila received a visit from the condo association's president, who gave her a warning and a fine for running a business from her home. She considered moving out and finding a place to live and run the studio, but between establishing Fawn and paying her normal expenses, Sheila was hemorrhaging money. She hadn't anticipated the cost of supplies and incidentals, like the new leggings, tanks, tunics, and hairbands she had felt compelled to buy when she realized that her yoga wardrobe was limited compared to that of most of her students, and that constant wear had left her gear looking dated and ragged. The one expense she was glad she had maintained was COBRA, especially after an MRI on her shoulder revealed three significant tears in her rotator cuff.

"Looks like you're out of the game," said the Orthopedist who evaluated her shoulder. "You took something way too far. Let's get you set with some PT."

Sheila sent a final email blast notifying students about the closure of Fawn, effective immediately. The physical therapist had forbidden her from practicing, but she tried anyway. Attempting even the simplest asanas brought tears to her eyes. Even eagle pose. Even down dog. Sheila called the partner who'd supervised her work at the firm.

"Tell you what," he said. "I can get you on conditionally. You'll start back on Jeff's team." Jeff was the colleague who had gleefully picked up the ball she'd dropped in the weeks before she left.

"Anything. Put me anywhere for anything. Thank you."

"Don't make me sorry I did this, champ."

"I promise you won't be sorry you did this."

Sheila donated all of the professional trappings of Fawn to the Episcopal church's recreations program and asked Lauren to return a few of the dresses and suits she'd given her so that she could go back to work at least looking like her old self. After meditating on her experience, she grudgingly admitted to herself that she had cultivated some gratitude for the parts of her life that hadn't completely fallen apart. She had a roof and a car and the beginnings of a job. Most of her body still worked perfectly, and her shoulder would mend. The night before she went back to work, she dug an abandoned pair of running shoes out of the back of her closet and made a slow two-mile loop around the track at the park near her condo. As she walked back to her car, feeling sweaty and at peace and wholly alive, she thought, *I could do this every day.*

Axilla

Rachel found a tunnel under her arm one morning.

The alarm clock read five fifteen. In thirty minutes, she would be making coffee, and then a peanut butter and grape jelly sandwich to wrap in foil and take to work. She closed her eyes and waited for the snooze to sound when she heard a thumping, firm and insistent. She switched on the television, expecting a weather map of Fayetteville clotted with bright orange or pink, whatever color indicated a massive thunderstorm. Nothing. She threw the covers off and looked out the bedroom window. The street. She was pulling on her robe when she realized the sound was coming from inside her body. She searched her ribs and chest with flattened palms, and then began to dig with her thumb into the soft flesh of her right armpit.

Rachel was able to push her whole hand into the space, and at the end of her reach, she found an elastic glob of what felt like mucus. *Good thing I took my watch off before bed,* she thought. She turned on the lamp at her bedside and sat on top of the covers to examine what she had found. It was purplish and alive with circulation, and as she brought it closer to her eyes, she could feel the threads of the thing's attachment to its source deep in her torso break away gently, like Velcro being pulled apart. As the stuff cooled in her palm, her boyfriend Peter began to stir in bed and lick his lips. She pushed her full fist back into her armpit and released the glob into the waiting space. The skin knit itself into place and she glanced at her hand. It was dry, and there was nothing left of what she found. Rachel placed her hand on her forehead. Normal, cool. She kissed Peter's cheek. "Are you alright?" she asked. "Do you feel alright?" Peter made an *mmmmm* sound and turned over. Rachel decided that she wasn't awake quite yet, she was still dreaming. She decided that her allergies were acting up and that she shouldn't take Benadryl at night, especially right before her period. She called in sick and made a cup of green tea instead of coffee.

96

Rachel's sleep was disturbed after that. Each night she as she unconsciously stretched her arms under her pillow or over her head, the thumping would jerk her awake, and she was able to reach inside for the glob again. Sex got weird after Peter's fingers accidentally slipped inside her chest, close to where her ribs began, as he rocked above her with his elbows dug into the mattress. She was close when she felt his fingers melting into to the flesh as it separated, until they were resting on a fascia-covered bone, exposed and beginning to emerge in the lamplight. Peter's eyes were closed in concentration, and the room was quiet, except for their breathing.

"I want to finish on top, okay?"

Peter opened his eyes. "Since when?"

"Since right now." Rachel rolled on top and the circuit of her underarm was broken. She clamped Peter's hands into the soft pockets of fat over her hips, and he pulled and she pushed and she came and then he came, the cleavage made by her bicep and ribcage as tight as a line drawn with a sharpened number two pencil.

Rachel and Peter went to a wedding a couple of days after the armpit fiasco began. She was stir crazy from being cooped up at home all week, wasting vacation days fretting over her weird body. She had sent Peter to his own apartment so that he couldn't discover her situation. What would he do if he knew? She imagined some kind of stoned-in-town-square scenario, or maybe a padded room.

There was a zydeco band at the wedding reception, and she and Peter each drank a couple of strong whiskey and Cokes. The drinks made them want to dance, which Rachel was enjoying until he spun her twice and a cascade of black jelly beans fell out of the short sleeve of her dress onto the tile patio. Rachel was so surprised by their ping and bounce that she tiptoed back abruptly in her high heels to avoid slipping or smashing a bunch of them into the soles of her sandals. Peter looked surprised, but as he pulled her back into him, Rachel realized that he had not seen the jelly beans fall out of her body. *I'm just drunk*, Rachel told herself. *I have just had too much to drink, and everything is fine.*

"I thought I saw something on the ground," she said, and laid her head on Peter's chest. "Some black stuff, some little black balls."

He glanced down at their feet, "I don't see anything. Probably just mosquitos, you know they love me. Are you having a good time?"

"I'm pretty drunk. Yes, I'm having fun."

Peter drove Rachel home after midnight, and she didn't ask him in. She was afraid that she was either really sick or suffering from the onset of serious mental illness, and pondering both options had effectively squelched her desire to get laid. She left her party clothes in a pile beside the bed, climbed in, and passed out. Her full bladder woke her up a couple of hours later. She hadn't pulled the curtains completely closed and when she returned from the bathroom, she encountered her own sleeping body, illuminated by a shaft of streetlight fluorescence. Her left leg was hitched up and to the side, and she noticed a long hair growing from her anklebone resting stiffly at the side of the foot. *That doesn't look right.* She brushed it with her fingers; it wasn't a hair. She aimed the alarm clock's glow at it and saw that it was a red waxen thread growing out of a pore among the light brown hair on her legs. She pulled at it, and it gave, the thread becoming longer as her skin released it. The releasing made a crisp sound like brittle paper being torn in two. The thread slit an open space along the side of her body, dark and bloodless, as her back expanded and contracted with the deep breath of sleep, tracing an opening up and over the crown of her head that ended at the bony ledge of the shoulder on her body's other side. The thread sprang away from its origin with a faint *pop*, leaving Rachel holding the slack end of all six and a half feet of it. *This is fucked up.* The dreamy alarm she had previously felt when her body went haywire had become a cold, pointed fear. She had unzipped herself, and now she had nowhere to live.

Rachel sat next to her own sleeping body and slid a hand beneath it, her palm at the tip of the sternum. She squeezed down on her back with her free hand positioned directly above, hoping the side would seal together as her armpit had before. She felt a light gush of air rush out of the space in her side, and the upper part of her body bounced away with a springiness and a *whoosh* that nauseated Rachel. Her face and arms were slick with icy perspiration as she slid her hands away and wiped them on her thighs. She patted the sheets for blood or fluid, but the bedding was dry.

A sound began in rhythm with her body's breath, a hollow thump beneath the right shoulder that grew louder and more insistent as its force increased, lifting the back of her body and letting it fall. Rachel stood beside the bed and watched as it lifted higher and higher until finally momentum flung it all back in one piece, and her body on the bed lay opened as a butterflied shrimp. Rachel leaned over to examine the inside. What she saw were not the orderly systems of organs she expected. The inside of her body looked like the ruined top of a pizza, the part that ends up stuck to the box, a petrified forest of bone-colored stalagmites mired in an orangey-red, viscous slush. *My insides look like leftovers*, she thought.

The thumping's source was a translucent purple dome the size of a baseball that lay in the place where the middle lobe of her right lung belonged. It pulsed from inside with lavender light in time with the sounds it emitted. Rachel recognized it as the goo she had pulled from inside her chest that first morning. Clustered around the dome were piles of the black orbs Rachel had seen at the wedding. She crooked an index finger around one and fished it out. She squeezed it and smelled. Licorice. She poked at the dome with the same finger's nail, and then it opened and she was standing inside.

A room with a fireplace set into one curved wall, the inside of the dome reminded Rachel of a picture she had seen once of a tiny dwelling carved into the side of a mountain in Greece, a crag of rock where some deified sage had rolled out his blanket. A clutch of dry kindling lay on the packed earth floor next to the fireplace. The noises, she saw, had been produced by the pointed end of a broomstick held by a woman crouched on the seat of a flowered armchair, the only furniture in the place. She jabbed at the dome's upper curve as if it were the ceiling of an apartment. *Her neighbors must be heavy walkers*, Rachel thought. *Her neighbors are my rotator cuff muscles*, she remembered next. *I am losing my mind right now.*

The woman was older than Rachel, about sixty. She wore a housecoat and slippers, and her black hair hung in two stiff braids that reached her elbows. She stepped heavily from the chair, bracing herself with the broom handle, and then shoved the broom at Rachel. She pointed at the fire and then at the chair. The woman shoved the chair aside, revealing a pile of the black jelly beans, which scattered wildly as they were exposed to the light.

"Sweep all of these into the fire," the woman said, pointing at the pile, "right now." She stood aside as Rachel began to sweep the jelly beans into the flames. Rachel could feel the woman's eyes on her as she worked, the candy melting into a waxen mess on the ashes before her. Sweeping faster caused the jelly beans to roll farther into the dark corners of the room. The woman noticed.

"Slow down and do it right."

The woman waited while Rachel chased every one of the jelly beans into the fire, and then she took the broom from her and moved the chair back into place. "Get up here now," she pointed at the cushion, "start at the ear."

Rachel stood on the cushion and accepted the broom. The woman motioned for her to bang at the ceiling as she had been doing when Rachel arrived. Rachel began to thump the ceiling. "Like this?" she asked.

"Hard as you can."

A crack appeared as Rachel thumped away at what felt like hard plastic above her head. Pieces of the dome fell to the floor around her, and when she had broken open a space the size of a hubcap, the woman stopped her. She reached for the broom, which she let clatter to the floor when Rachel handed it over. The woman stood beside the chair and took a folded piece of paper from the pocket of her housecoat. She handed the paper to Rachel and clasped her hands to make a place for Rachel's foot.

"Wait. No." The woman raised her eyebrows at Rachel.

"There is something you should know," the woman raised her chin at the dregs of licorice and wood in the fireplace and then grabbed at Rachel's ankle. "Now get up there. You will see the brain from the ear. That note goes in the big space at the back of the brain. Only one space is empty, so no problem. Get in and put your hands up."

The woman was strong. She boosted Rachel through the ceiling space. Rachel's fingers brushed the end of a rope, and she tried to grab hold with the hand that wasn't holding the paper. She landed flat on her ass in the armchair. "One more chance," the woman said. "Do it right this time." Rachel clamped the paper in her teeth and raised her hands again.

The rope began to swing as Rachel grasped it, and her toes bumped against a hard shelf at the top of the swinging. She arched her back and launched herself onto a ledge, a foot-wide stone jutting backed by a spongy wall.

"Turn around." The lady's voice echoed up from beneath the ledge. A dim shaft of light from the fire inside the dome revealed four rough-hewn wooden steps leading to a pile of stones stacked into a loose, sloppy wall. Slips of paper were wedged in the open spaces, some with ragged edges, and others as stiff and flat as index cards. "Look for the space in the back," she heard from below. Rachel removed the paper from her mouth.

"I still need to get to the brain," Rachel shouted. "This is just a wall."

"That's it. That's the brain."

"No."

"Yes. Find the space in the back and deliver that message."

Rachel unfolded the paper. The message read: *Under new ownership.*

Rachel found the large space on the far side of the wall and inserted the folded paper there. Nearby, a scrap of yellow legal pad, rolled in a tube, caught her eye. She decided against asking to read the message. The woman might have told her to mind her own business. She pinched the edge with her thumb and forefinger and eased it from its space. It said: *Cracks in foundation.*

Rachel began pulling out papers, one after another. An acid green post-it, the sticky side folded under: *Shingles.* A receipt from Tucker's Speedy Oil Exchange: *Stop telling people about your abortion.* Torn loose-leaf: *Ask for three thousand more.*

She wadded all the papers into one large crack and called down, "Is there another way out?"

"You're lazy. Turn around and move yourself. One way in, one way out."

Rachel landed hard on her feet on the dome's dirt floor.

"I suppose you want an explanation," the woman said. "Do you know what intuition is?"

"Of course —"

"It is something you lack. I am yours. I am your intuition and I am retiring. I will be off duty forever at the end of July. Today is the first. Now you do."

The woman's name was Judith. She met Rachel in the dome for the next thirty nights, no breaks. Every time, the same unzipping, the jelly beans, the wall. Sweeping away the candy that seemed to regenerate itself anew each night frustrated her the most.

"Why jelly beans? I don't even like licorice."

"Those are not jelly beans. Those are the decisions you refused to make, even with my help. You let someone else make all of those decisions for you. I had to find place to put those, and candy is easy to bundle up and stow away. I kept most of them where your tonsils used to be. They are small, but there are so many. Fix that."

"What kind of small decisions?"

"At least fifty percent of them are about eating. You have spent plenty of time agonizing over where to go to put food your mouth. Keep sweeping."

Rachel's next task was to organize and clear away all of the old messages stuck in the wall. Judith gave Rachel two cardboard shoeboxes and told her to smooth each paper and file it in the appropriate box. One was marked "happy," the other, "sad."

"These papers cannot stay," Judith instructed, handing Rachel the boxes when she had finished filling them up. "They belong elsewhere. Take sad to the space behind your right knee. Put happy in the pocket located on the left side of your navel." She stamped her foot twice and Rachel fell through the dome's floor.

Her knee was a cold and windy space that Rachel could not wait to escape. The navel was warmer, if a bit tight. She had to elbow at the walls to fit inside, and as she nestled the box into a pocket there, she wondered how she would get back into the dome. She glanced up at the roof, but there was no broom to break it open. It occurred to her that the way she got in might have something to do with the way she'd get out, so she stamped her own foot twice and she was back in the dome, in front of Judith.

"Good for you. Now get to work on that wall."

Rachel had to pry the stones loose one at a time, starting at the top. She had to take apart her entire brain and set it right another way, "Any way you want." This took five whole nights, and when she had finished, Judith asked her to stand in front of what she had made, a maze of rocks in the design of a honeycomb, with hundreds of generous spaces, the opposite of the precarious looking anthill of consciousness that had existed there before.

"That's nice and neat." Judith handed her a new pad of sticky notes. "To get you started."

"Thanks, I tried to keep it low to the ground. The other one looked dangerous."

About the Author

Jane V. Blunschi holds an MFA in Fiction Writing from the University of Arkansas. Her travel book, *Love, Tupelo* was published in 2012 by Corvus Press, and she was a Lambda Literary Fellow in 2014. Her work has been featured in or is forthcoming from *Cactus Heart Literary Magazine, Catahoula Zine, Paper Darts* and *Sun Star Review*. Originally from Lafayette, Louisiana, Jane lives in Fayetteville, Arkansas.

Acknowledgements

Grateful acknowledgment is made to the publishers of the following publications, in which these stories first appeared, some in slightly different form.

Gaslight: "Snapdragon"
Paper Darts: "Sheena"
Sun Star Review: "Porcelain Doves"
Cactus Heart Literary Review: "Axilla"

The title of this collection is a lyric from the song "Let's Get It On" by Marvin P. Gaye and Ed Townsend.

I am so grateful and honored that Yellow Flag Press chose this collection for publication. J. Bruce Fuller and Scott Thomason: Thank you for your unflagging energy and attention to detail. Thank you for believing in my work.

My teachers and colleagues in the MFA program at the University of Arkansas provided me with the fellowship, encouragement, and honest criticism I needed to make these stories come alive. Thank you all.

I'd also like to thank the Lambda Literary Foundation and my cohort of fellows. Knowing you all has made such an important difference in my life.

Most of all, I'd like to thank my number one, Steph Shinabery.

~ The Cypress & Pine Fiction Series ~

Series Editor: W. Scott Thomason

Titles in the Series

2017
Understand Me, Sugar
Jane V. Blunschi